"So, wh⸺ ⸺ ⸺ ⸺ your life?" I asked.

"I'm not really sure yet," Chuck admitted. "I do know I want to have my own business. Only what sort of business, I don't know. What about you?"

"I guess I'm like you—" We had stopped walking, and I stood facing him, wanting to tell him about my idea of having a real catering business. But I wondered if he'd think I was silly. I decided not to share my dream for a while longer. "I guess I'll just wait to find out what I want to do, too," I said.

Chuck didn't say anything for a moment. He was still looking at me, his head bent, the moonlight highlighting his unruly hair.

"I know what I want to do right now," Chuck finally said, his voice low and suddenly rumbly. Slowly he began to pull me toward him, tilting his head farther down as he gently pressed his mouth against mine.

Two's A Crowd

Diana Gregory

BANTAM BOOKS

TORONTO · NEW YORK · LONDON · SYDNEY · AUCKLAND

RL 6, IL age 11 and up

TWO'S A CROWD
A Bantam Book/August 1985

*Sweet Dreams and its associated logo are registered trademarks of
Bantam Books, Inc. Registered in U.S. Patent and Trademark Office
and elsewhere.*

Cover photo by Pat Hill.

ISBN 0-553-24992-4

Published simultaneously in the United States and Canada

---

*Bantam Books are published by Bantam Books, Inc. Its trademark,
consisting of the words "Bantam Books" and the portrayal of
a rooster, is Registered in U.S. Patent and Trademark Office
and in other countries. Marca Registrada. Bantam Books, Inc.,
666 Fifth Avenue, New York, New York 10103.*

Printed and bound in Great Britain by
Cox & Wyman Ltd, Reading

O   0 9 8 7 6 5 4 3 2 1

Two's A Crowd

Chapter One

Lying flat on my back, I stared up at the bottom of my car. We, it and I, were near the intersection of Oak and Grand, where the car had clunked to a halt minutes before. A blob of black goo bubbled out of what had to be one of its major working parts. I had a strong feeling this wasn't supposed to be happening. The blob grew bigger, shimmered, and dropped onto my chin, before I could move. I disregarded the sound of a truck starting and then stopping again very close to my car. All I could think of was a big, fat garage bill.

"Hey, down there," a voice echoed through the open hood. "Need some help?"

"I jerked upward and banged my head on the thing that was oozing black.

1

"Was that a yes?"

I looked up through the maze of engine parts, but all I could see was part of a very tanned male arm.

"What did you say?" the voice echoed again.

"Go away," I said. I was really upset and didn't want to talk to anyone, least of all some strange male person who wanted to prove how terrific he was at fixing my car. Don't get me wrong. I'm not antimale, but it gets me mad when one of them looks upon a female as being totally incapable of handling anything mechanical.

He evidently hadn't heard me because he hollered down again. I swiveled my head to one side in the hope of making myself understood and came face to face with a pair of grungy, ancient sneakers. I decided to direct my answer to them.

"I don't want any help. Thank you."

"Are you sure?"

This time I didn't answer. I just closed my eyes and decided if I didn't say anything else the person with the grungy sneakers and the tanned arm would just disappear.

"Well, then," he persisted, "if you don't need any help, would you please move your car? It's blocking the drive, and I can't get my truck out."

2

What drive? What was he talking about? I looked past the sneakers. It was there. I hadn't noticed it before. But there it was. A truck painted hot pink. What kind of a guy drove a hot pink truck?

"Hey, miss. Are you OK down there?"

"Yes."

"Well, I wasn't sure. You weren't answering."

I sighed.

"Hello?"

"Oh, all right. You're right," I admitted.

"About what?"

"That I need help."

"Too bad."

Too bad? What did that mean? Scooting on my bottom, worm-fashion, I inched out from beneath the car. Almost instantly two strong hands grabbed mine and hauled me the rest of the way out and to my feet. There I was, my hands still being held, looking into a pair of the most perfect, bluest eyes I had ever seen. Gradually I took in the rest of him. Dark blond lashes fringed the perfect eyes. And he had a perfect tan, too, as if he'd spent the entire summer just lying on the beach. Only the hair falling down on his forehead ruined the perfect image. It was a little too sun bleached and casual—almost to the point of being messy. He let go of my hands and pushed at his hair. But as soon as he'd stopped pushing, it fell right back over his forehead.

When he said "Hi," the bottom half of his face creased into a wide grin.

I said "Hi!" back and silently read the name printed across the pocket of his shirt. "Diaper Dan?" I asked.

"Right!" He bowed slightly. "At least from four to six on Tuesday and Friday afternoons, plus all day on Saturday. Otherwise, I'm known as Charles Whitford, Jr., Chuck to my friends. And what do your friends call you?"

"Peggy. Peggy Jenkins." I tipped my head, looking at him. For some reason he suddenly seemed familiar. "Do I know you?"

"Do you swim?"

"Well, sure, but what has that got to do with knowing you?"

"I was a lifeguard at King's Lake this summer. If you ever swam there, you probably noticed me in the same way you noticed the shack or the picnic tables or the trash cans—they're there, but you don't pay much attention to them."

"You're crazy, Chuck Whitford," I said, laughing. "I hardly spent any time at the beach at all this summer. I'm sure I would have remembered you if I had seen you."

"I won't press my luck by asking why. I'll

just take it as a compliment," he said. "Anyway, I don't live around here. I only come to Gardnerville in the guise of Diaper Dan. The real Chuck Whitford lives in Morton, a fast twenty minutes in my van, or a slow thirty-five in the Diapermobile."

"The Diapermobile!" I smiled. "I don't know what your van looks like, but I think I'd choose it over the Diapermobile any day."

"Me, too," Chuck replied.

"Have you noticed we match?" Chuck asked, pointing at my sweat shirt.

I was dressed for the Saturday aerobics class I was now missing, in tights and a sweat shirt with The Sweat Shop printed across the front.

"We're both wearing pink," Chuck said. "Except your shirt is covered in black dots." He leaned forward and wiped at my chin.

"Oh, no," I moaned, remembering the black glop from the bottom of the car. "I must look horrible!" I held out my filth-covered hands.

"Yeah," Chuck agreed. "You're pretty much of a mess all right." Hauling a torn blue bandanna from the back pocket of his jeans, he handed it to me.

"Thanks," I said. "For the use of the bandanna, I mean."

"You're welcome," he answered, giving

the now greasy rag a slightly disgusted look and stuffing it back into his hip pocket. "I'll keep it just this way so I can remember this day forever."

"Oh, sorry," I apologized. "I guess I should offer to wash it and mail it back to you."

"Forget it." The corners of his blue eyes crinkled as he smiled. "Like I said, it's now a cherished memento."

"Well—"

"I hate to break this up, but I think we'd better do something about getting your car moving again. Because if I don't get the Diapermobile out of this driveway and back into action, there might very well be a wet baby bottom crisis in Gardnerville. Worse than that, I could get fired for dereliction of duty."

"I'm sorry. I wasn't thinking."

"Any idea what's wrong with it?"

"Nope. It just died."

"Well, how did it die? I mean, did it make a death rattle or just stop?"

"Well, there was a noise, kind of like an earthquake. I figured I'd run over something and it had gotten caught underneath for just a second. You know, like when you run over a can and it bounces around. That's why I crawled under the car. I thought that if something was stuck, I could get it loose."

6

"Right." Chuck nodded. "Did you happen to notice anything actually dropping off your car?"

OK, so I had to admit he sounded as if he knew what he was talking about. Maybe this was the time to allow the supposed superiority of male mechanical ability to come ahead of my dislike of being made to feel incompetent. And, after all, it seemed only logical that if he could save someone's life, he could certainly aid my car. But, when I looked down at Chuck's hands, they didn't look like they'd spent much time tinkering with greasy nuts and bolts. Nevertheless, I asked, "Do you think something might have fallen off?"

"When you were under there, did it look as though anything was missing?"

"I really wouldn't know," I said, shaking my head. "Do you want to take a look for yourself?"

"Not really. I don't think it would do much good."

I suddenly got worried. Was there something more seriously wrong than I'd imagined? And was he trying to break the news to me gently? "What do you mean?" I asked finally.

"I mean, I just wouldn't know if there was anything really missing. I'm not into cars.

Now if you were drowning, I probably could save you. I'm a great lifeguard."

"Then why did you ask me all those questions?"

"Well, I thought that maybe with the two of us discussing it, we might figure out the problem."

"Oh, great!" My hope crumpled and with it my good feelings about Chuck Whitford. "Why don't you just go back to delivering your diapers," I said, though not unkindly.

"I'd love to," Chuck answered. "But I can't. Your car is still in the way, in case you forgot."

Now I felt foolish—and confused and angry as well. "Why did you act as if you knew exactly what you were doing?"

Chuck looked hurt. "I was going to try to help. There are some things I know about. You could have a dead battery, for instance. I know what to do about that."

"So do I." My pride took hold, and the words came out more harshly than I intended. "I also know how to change spark plugs and my oil filter."

"Really? That's more than I know."

His admission made me feel even worse about the way I was acting. After all, he was trying to help.

Chuck walked around to the front of the

car and bent over the engine compartment. Reaching in, he jiggled a wire.

"I thought you didn't know anything about cars," I said and looked in to see which wire he was jiggling.

He didn't answer, just jiggled the wire again.

"Well?"

"Right!" He stopped jiggling it, reached up, and slammed the hood down.

"I could've done that," I said, laughing.

"But can you push this car and steer at the same time?"

"No," I admitted.

"Then it's time for team spirit. You get in and steer while I push." He motioned with his head. "Just up there about twenty feet, in that fifteen-minute parking zone."

"I'll get a ticket if I park there," I protested.

"Do you have a choice?"

I shook my head.

"Then get in the car. Unless, of course, you'd rather push."

Minutes later, sitting beside Chuck in the Diapermobile, I glanced in the rearview mirror on my side of the truck and watched my little yellow Honda get smaller. The square of white paper Chuck had stuck under the windshield wiper was flapping in the breeze. He'd penciled a note to anyone who might be concerned—a policeman, for instance—that the car was parked in a fifteen-minute zone only until it could be moved. I was glad he'd thought to do that. He might not know a lot about cars, but he certainly knew about some other important things. He was good-looking, too. His face was strong, with a high, intelligent forehead above the perfect eyes. "Thank you for taking time to drive me to a gas station," I said, wanting him to know I did appreciate what he was doing.

"Sure. No sweat." Chuck turned and gave me a quick smile. "Don't worry about the car; it'll probably be fixed and back working by this afternoon."

He dodged around a slow-moving, older sedan but was stopped by a red light. "There's a good-sized Shell station on the next corner. I've heard the service department is halfway decent. OK with you?"

"Sure, I suppose." I shrugged. "One station is as good as another. Aren't they all expensive? Anyway, I can't ask you to keep driving me around town when you're supposed to be delivering diapers."

Half an hour later as we drove out of the station, Chuck was trying to make me feel better about what I'd heard. "The mechanic's probably wrong," he said. "It doesn't necessarily have to be the transmission. Maybe it's just some little bolt that's fallen off. You said you heard something funny."

"No. It can't be that simple," I said, slumping into the seat and staring unhappily out through the windshield. "It never is."

Chuck kept trying to comfort me, but nothing he said made any difference.

"The real problem," I said, staring morosely ahead, "is that I don't have the money to pay for some expensive repair job. I've got just enough in my bank account to cover my next insurance premium. Which is due very soon."

"Don't you have a job?" Chuck asked.

"Job?"

"Don't tell me. I know. You've got doting parents who foot your every bill, right? But you just don't want to disappoint them by telling them that the car they bought for you collapsed on the street."

"I bought the car myself," I said, fixing him with a stare. "I worked all last year and this summer to get it. And I saved enough for the insurance, too. I just didn't count on something like this happening. And I don't have a job right now."

"How'd you earn the money for the car?" Chuck asked, ignoring my glare.

"Baby-sitting," I answered. And seeing a

11

smile starting at the corner of his mouth, I added, "Believe me, it was hard work. This summer I looked after a set of triplets, all day, five days a week. Which is enough to give any-one nervous fits. And I can see why their mother chose to go back to work full-time."

"What about gas?" Chuck went on.

"Baby-sitting again," I answered. "Just the regular kind. Evenings."

"Maybe your answer is to get a real job," Chuck suggested. "Take me. You don't think I deliver diapers because it gives me a thrill to drive around in a hot pink truck, do you?"

"Well, no," I answered. "But I hadn't really thought very much about why you were doing it."

"For my van. It costs a mint to keep going. But it's definitely worth it. I wouldn't give up that van for anything. Besides," he said shoot-ing me a glance, "most girls don't like to date guys who only take them places on the bus."

The way he said it, I wanted to tell him it wasn't true, that girls don't really care about whether guys have cars or not. But thinking about my friends, I knew he was right. "I guess that's one of those facts of life."

"Yeah, life's tough all over," Chuck said.

"I don't suppose Dan's Diaper Service could use another driver, could they?"

"Not at the moment. But if I can ever find

something else I can do to make the bucks, there'll be an opening. Not that I would recommend the job to anyone. Dan's not exactly up for boss of the year. You might term him a louse."

"And you're taking a chance on getting fired by driving me home?"

"Like I said, my route's fairly close to where you live, and I can make up time on my deliveries."

"What kind of job are you looking for?" I asked, curious.

"Anything!" Chuck answered. "Well, actually anything where I can be my own boss. I don't mind hard work. In fact, I'm a workaholic. It's just that I don't like working for someone else."

He paused long enough to make the right-hand turn onto my street. "Only problem is that, other than being a great lifeguard, being capable of finding addresses all over town, and managing to maintain an OK average in school, my only real talent is being able to put together a fantastic bowl of Texas chili."

"That's where I live," I said pointing to a white, turn-of-the-century house halfway down the block.

"OK," he said. Pulling up at the curb, Chuck put the truck in park and threw his arm casually over the back of my seat. "So you see, I guess I'd better stick to being Diaper Dan for a while."

"I guess you're right," I agreed. I could feel the heat of his fingers as they almost touched my shoulder. "And I guess I'd better stick to my baby-sitting. My talents aren't exactly extensive either. I play a mean game of Candyland and slap jack, plus I do a great chocolate cake. But that's about it."

"If that chocolate cake's from scratch, that sounds pretty talented to me." Chuck's fingers accidently rippled the material of my sweat shirt, and a wide grin spread across his face. "But I guess no one's going to beat a path to our respective doors for your cake or my chili."

"Right," I said, feeling little goose bumps rise. "Well, thanks a lot for driving me home. I mean it. I really hope you don't get in trouble for doing it."

"Don't worry," he said with assurance. "I'll make my deliveries faster and push this tank up to the speed limit on the way back to Morton. And if Dan does get on my case, I'll just remind myself it was worth it."

"Worth it?" I suddenly felt myself starting to blush.

"Sure!" he answered seriously, but there was a hint of a smile on his face. "It isn't every day I get to rescue a car."

"Oh, that," I answered, feeling stupid and embarrassed because I'd jumped to the conclusion it was because he'd met me. To cover my blush, I turned and shoved down the door handle.

"Well," I said, ready to make the break, "thanks again, Chuck."

"No problem." He gave me a friendly smile. "Anytime you and your car get into trouble, just look for the Diaper Dan truck."

"I hope that's not too soon," I called as he began to pull away. The minute I said that I wanted to take back the words. Because what I really hoped was that I'd see Diaper Dan again soon, very soon.

Chapter Two

"That's really too bad," Mom said sympathetically. She finished peeling another apple, sliced it into neat slivers, and plopped the slivers into a bowl of cold water that was standing on the counter.

Folding a towel and adding it to the pile of already folded towels on the table, I nodded silently. "It's just that I only have so much money in my savings account," I moaned, automatically picking up another towel from the laundry basket and beginning to fold it, too.

It had been nearly four hours since Chuck had dropped me off at home. I still hadn't heard from the man at the Shell station, and the longer the wait, the more positive I was that the costs were adding up.

"Maybe it's as that young man Chuck said, that the repairs won't be as bad as you're thinking."

"I could let my insurance go for just a little while so I could pay the bill," I suggested. "I know lots of kids at school who are driving around without insurance because it costs too much."

"I don't think your father would approve of that idea," Mom said. She picked up another apple and studied it. "And, quite frankly, neither would I. I'm truly sorry. I wish I could help. But you know all the money I earn goes to pay off our second mortgage."

I could tell she didn't like having to say this. But Mom is a realist. Ever since I've been old enough to understand about these things, she's been honest about family finances.

"I know, Mom. I honestly understand."

She reached for a towel to dry her hands. "Maybe it's just some little nut or bolt that fell off."

"I'd like to think so, Mom," I said. "But I really don't." The laundry was all folded. I put the stacks neatly back into the basket so that I could carry them upstairs to put into the linen closet. "Are you making brown betty or apple pie?"

"Apple pie," Mom said. "Your father's been a bit on the grouchy side lately. Some kind of problem out at the plant. Nothing major. But I thought having his favorite dessert might make him feel better for a little while. Meat loaf, too."

"In that case, I'll put the laundry away before you ask me to chop the onions for the meat loaf. I have a feeling I'm going to have enough reason to cry without chopping onions to do it."

It was nearly five before the man from the service station called. I stopped listening after he'd given me the total cost. He went on, talking about replacement parts and rebuilt gizmos. But he could have been reciting the Gettysburg Address for all I cared. If I gave him everything in my savings account, I'd still owe him $26.79.

At the dinner table, despite the warning glances Mom gave me, I broached the subject about delaying my insurance payment for a while. I have to admit, my father didn't explode. He simply reached for more meat loaf and shook his head at the same time.

"Please, Dad?"

"No!" He smiled over at Mom. "This is really great meat loaf, honey."

"But, Dad," I continued to plead, "I'll drive

very carefully. And I'll only drive when it's absolutely necessary. Like to school and back, and to my aerobics class. And maybe to Tami's and back."

"No way, Peggy."

"But—"

"No!" This time Dad stopped eating and pointed his fork at me. "No one in this family ever drives so much as out of the driveway without insurance. Is that clear? And I really mean that."

"Yes, sir!" I said and scowled.

"And you needn't frown," Dad went on. "Try remembering back a few months when you decided you simply had to have a car and I told you that you'd better plan for emergencies as well. What'd you think I meant by an emergency, having to replace the seat covers because you were tired of the color of the old ones?"

"Well, no." I slumped back in my seat. Actually, I'd been asking Dad for new ones for my birthday.

Dad shoved his fork into his mashed potatoes, looked thoughtful for a moment, then laid the fork down. "Tell you what," he said, picking up his coffee cup. "You pay as much as you can of the service station bill with your savings, and I'll pay the balance of it, as well as advance you the money needed to pay your insurance." He took a swallow of coffee. "But—"

"Oh, Dad." I started to jump up so I could go around the table and hug him. "That's great!"

"Wait!" He held up a hand. "Just wait until you've heard the rest."

Sinking back down in my chair, I told myself I should have known it wouldn't be that easy.

"Here are my terms. You are to drive the car straight back here to the house from the station after it's fixed. Then it's to stay parked in the garage until you have completely and totally reimbursed me, both for the insurace and for the balance you need to pay off the repair bill. Is that agreed?"

"But—"

"Actually, Peggy," Dad went on, "you should be thanking me. I'm saving you from having to look for a new insurance company after the one you have now drops you when you let your premium lapse. And any new one would probably charge you more. That's the way things are in the real world." He gave me that I'm-an-adult-and-I-know look.

"Oh, wow," I said sarcastically.

"Peggy!" Mom raised an eyebrow.

"Well, Mom—"

"Peggy!"

"Thanks, Dad," I said, trying to sound grateful. But, I asked myself as I sank into my own thoughts, was I really any better off with his help? I guessed so, according to his rules. But I didn't feel that way.

As I cleared the table of the dinner plates and helped Mom serve the apple pie, I thought about Chuck Whitford. Dad would definitely approve of what he was doing. He was being a responsible, working, adult-type person, delivering diapers in order to support his van. I smiled to myself, remembering the Diaper Dan truck.

Well, OK, great, so he had a job as a delivery person. What could I do? Maybe I could find a job delivering pizza or something. But did I really want a job like that? My best friend, Tami, worked at Taco Pete's on Sundays to support her clothes habit. But I'd tried working at a fast-food place once and quit on the second day. It had paid the same as baby-sitting, and I'd come home so totally wiped out I'd gone to bed at five in the afternoon. So just what kind of a job was I supposed to find? Staring moodily at the piece of pie in front of me, I pushed at it with my fork and let my parents' conversation flow around me.

"Consequently," my father was saying, "with the new orders we're receiving, we're going to have to put on some weekend shifts."

"Oh, dear," Mom said. "Does that mean you'll have to work weekends as well? You put in such long hours now we barely ever see you."

"No." Dad shook his head. "Thank goodness I've got a new man I can rely on to be the weekend foreman. He's quite good. One of my problems now, though, is finding a catering service that will send out a lunch truck for the smaller crew. The catering service we have during the week has already said no. Not enough people to warrant a truck coming all the way out from town. And I can't just tell the men they'll have to brown-bag it. Telling them they were going to have to work weekends was hard enough."

"Have you called that other catering service over in Morton?"

"Yep!" Dad nodded. "But no go. They said the same thing. Not enough business to justify the distance."

"That's too bad," Mom said.

"So I thought maybe some of those food-dispensing machines might do for a while."

"Oh, Jack, really!" Mom served herself another small sliver of pie. "Talk about having your men upset. I can just imagine how they'd react if you did that."

"Just about what I thought, too," Dad said. "Probably cause a strike, or at least a

23

temporary walkout." He shook his head. "I'll just have to keep trying. Maybe there's a catering service I haven't thought of yet."

It was just like in the cartoons strips, as if a light bulb had suddenly gone on over my head. I actually looked up to see if it was there.

"Dad!"

"Hmm—what is it, Peggy?" Dad glanced over at me with a look as if he'd been so engrossed in his conversation with Mom that he'd almost forgotten I was still at the table.

"Dad . . ." I gulped air, excited so much by what I wanted to say that I couldn't seem to get it out.

"What is it, Peggy?" My father suddenly looked concerned. "Are you sick?"

"Dad—Dad!" My stomach was developing knots. "I'm your solution. I can do it."

"Do what, honey?" Dad's face still showed concern. But now there was confusion, too.

"I can do the catering service for you."

"Oh, now, Peggy—"

"No, I mean it," I broke in. "I can. Really! I make terrific sandwiches. You know I do. You're always telling me what a great sand-wich maker I am—"

"Peggy, honey, please," Dad interrupted. "I know you mean well. But I'm talking serious here. Sure you make great sandwiches. But, honey, one great sandwich does not a catering service make."

I didn't smile back. "Dad, please don't treat me like a little girl. I'm serious, too."

"Well, why not, Jack?" Mom's voice was tinged with excitement. I shot her a thankful glance.

"Well—" Dad hesitated. "Listen, you two, don't gang up on me." He threw up his hands. "I can see you really are serious, Peggy. And I'm sure you might feel, right this minute, that you would like to try something like that. And maybe you'd even last more than one weekend. But if you got bored after that and quit, it wouldn't sit well with the men. And I simply can't afford for that to happen. No," he said, shaking his head. "I think you'd better stick to baby-sitting."

"Jack Jenkins!" Mom said, shouting down Dad. "I think Peggy just might have a good idea. And I think you should be giving her credit for it." Dad looked at her in surprise. She went on. "Baby-sitting is fine for a fourteen-year-old, but Peggy's sixteen now. And, after all, she did earn the money for her own car this summer. Oh, I agree she didn't quite think out all the problems that go along with owning a car. But it seems to me that I remember that fifty-seven Chevy you had when we were going steady in high school.

And, if I remember right," she said, her eyes twinkling, "it was because the radiator cracked and you didn't have the money to get a new one that we took the bus to the junior prom."

My mouth flew open in surprise, and I tried not to make a sound as I glanced over at Dad.

"All right, all right," Dad said, looking embarrassed. "I think that's enough of our past. So, OK, Peggy, I'll hear your idea out. What you're proposing is a real business, you know."

"Yes, I know, Dad," I answered, finding that I was having trouble with my breathing again. "The truth is that my mind's racing with all sorts of ideas. So could we talk?"

"Isn't that what I just said?" Dad smiled.

"Oh, yeah, right!" I took a deep breath. *Calm down,* I told myself.

"So, it all boils down to having to take on the total responsibility," my father said, summing up everything the three of us had talked about for the past two hours. "And, as you've agreed, Peggy, I'll go ahead and advance you the money to pay both the car repair bill and your insurance, so you can use the money in your savings account as capital." He looked over at Mom. "Does everything sound fair to you?"

"Absolutely!" Mom agreed. "But how do you feel, Peggy?"

"I feel like"—I hesitated—"I've just become a businesswoman." Then I jumped up and ran to the table and planted a big kiss on the top of my father's bald spot. "I love you, Dad." I hugged him.

"I don't call that being very businesslike," Dad mumbled, but I noticed he wasn't complaining about the hug.

"So what are you going to call your catering service?" Mom asked.

"Well . . ." I tipped my head to one side, thinking. "How about Peggy's Lunches?"

"A good name," Mom said.

"A good name," Dad said, seconding Mom. "And an honest one." Then raising his coffee cup in a toast he announced, "Here's to Peggy's Lunches. And to success!"

Chapter Three

Tami closed the door to her locker and spun the combination. "I admire you, Peggy," she said as we started walking down the hall together, "but frankly, I think you're biting off a lot more than I'd ever want to chew."

I guess she was right—about herself. She was trying to show me just how the business would restrict my life.

"Look," I said, "you spend your Sundays working at Taco Pete's."

"But Sundays aren't Saturdays. Who dates on Sundays? And what about your aerobics class? Your muscles are going to get flabby." Before I could say anything, she asked, "How long did your father say you had to do this?"

"He didn't say I *had* to do it at all. I'm the one who talked him into letting me do it, remember? But right now it's only until I've paid him back and saved enough for what he calls an emergency fund for my car."

Since Tami was being so negative, I tried to change the subject. I started talking about Chuck Whitford, whom I had described, in detail, to her over the phone Sunday night. But she continued to be negative, even about Chuck.

"Just remember what I said on the subject of falling for guys who aren't local," she warned. "Long distance relationships do not work. Take my word for it!"

"You're an authority because one pen pal from seventh grade didn't work out for you?" I rolled my eyes.

"Nevertheless," Tami said, "I know about the pain such a relationship can cause."

"Anyway, about my catering business." I was determined to keep my thoughts positive. "If it works out the way I hope it will, my father has agreed that I can just keep it going. The weekend work crew out at the plant is permanent. Listen," I said and hugged my books at the thought, "I might end up so successful that Peggy's Lunches will turn into a full-time business."

"You're kidding!"

"No," I said. "Why would I kid about a thing like that?"

"Well, just spare me!" It was now Tami's turn to roll her eyes. "I can just see you with a fleet of those stainless steel lunch trucks! Please, Peggy, don't get carried away by this little venture."

"That wasn't exactly the way I'd been thinking," I replied, trying not to sound too deflated. After all, I'd spent all of Sunday dreaming about what Peggy's Lunches could become. "See, I sort of thought that I could take the business one step more, and after I got really successful with what I'm going to do out at the plant, I could turn it into one of those chic catering companies, the ones that do private parties and important social events."

"And just when do you plan on doing this chic catering? On weekends?" Tami shook her head. "I think those businesses have to be full time. People have parties on weekdays as well as weekends."

"Well, actually, I was thinking about doing that after I grad—"

Tami grabbed my arm, stopping me in midsentence. "Excuse me, Peggy, but this is my class, and I've got to go right in. There's this adorable new guy, and I want to show him Gardnerville High students are friendly. I'm going to ask him if he needs any help finding his way around." She batted her eyelashes playfully.

"So now you're playing Welcome Wagon lady?" I said, laughing.

"Only because I can't get Lon Chambers who spends every spare second drooling over you. I swear, Peggy," Tami said and shook her head, "that's another thing. I would give my two cashmere sweaters for one date with Lon. And you act as if he's a first cousin with warts. What gives?"

"What can I say? Lon's nice, and I admit he is pretty fantastic looking. But it just seems as though I've known him forever. When we date now, there just isn't the excitement that there used to be."

"Well," Tami said, grinning wickedly, "it wouldn't take very much for Lon Chambers to excite me." She backed toward the open door, campaign tactics already clear in her eyes. "Hey, see you at lunch!"

"Bye!" I said, laughing and shaking my head.

Study hall is my first period. That's normally when I do most of my homework. But that day I'd planned on doing some more thinking about my new business. I had lists to make and a budget to set down. I was going to prove to my dad just how responsible I could be.

I entered the classroom and slipped into my seat, then took out my ballpoint pen and a sheet of ruled notebook paper. I nibbled on the end of the pen. Tami hadn't allowed me to finish what I was going to tell her, which was what I'd been thinking about all day Sunday. Until I'd come up with the idea Saturday night, I'd just been wandering through life, through high school without any motivation. I was taking college prep classes, but I still hadn't decided which college I wanted to attend, or even what I wanted to major in. Now I knew; all the pieces fell into place. I said to myself, "Peggy Jenkins, this is what you want to do with your life." The thought of running a really successful catering business seemed terribly exciting.

Leaning over my note paper, I began writing down columns of figures. And after that I began making a list of everything I was going to need. I was determined to succeed.

By Thursday I was pretty well organized. My car was fixed and, as the man from the station said, as good as new again. Or at least as new as any five-year-old car with 63,999 miles on the odometer and a dented left front fender could be.

After school Tami and I drove across town to the Grab and Bag Warehouse, a place that sells food at nearly wholesale rates and carries restaurant-sized staple items, such as gallon jars of mayonnaise and mustard. Mom suggested buying my staples that way. Otherwise, she'd said, my margin of profit would be too small.

I left my car in the store parking lot, and Tami and I went inside. The place was like no other market I'd ever seen. Instead of things being displayed neatly on shelves, there were cartons of cans and jars just stacked every which way along double width aisles. Tami and I pushed two oversize carts up and down, filling them with giant jars of pickles, mayonnaise, mustard, and twenty-pound packages of sliced cheeses and luncheons meats, as well as about forty other things that were on my list.

Thirty minutes later, back in the front seat of the car, the rear filled with brown bags stuffed with my purchases, I looked at the rolled grocery slip. "Tami," I asked, "do you know how much money I've just spent?"

Tami leaned over, checked the total, and whistled. "Wow! That's the same as that gorgeous red coat you've been drooling over at Mervyn's. And to think that by tomorrow afternoon it's all going to have been eaten up by a horde of hungry men."

"Well," I said, grinning, "I guess that's the basic idea."

"I guess so." Tami smiled happily. "Then you'll have made so much money, you'll be able to buy the coat outright instead of having to put it on layaway."

"But only after I've paid my father off first," I reminded her. Then giving my flattened wallet a resigned glance, I suggested, "Want to go to Burger King? I think I have just enough for fries and a drink."

"Aren't you supposed to be driving straight home? I mean, no detours."

"Burger King isn't detouring," I said. "It *is* on the way home. So I think that makes it legally OK."

"Oh, all right." Tami laughed. "Sure. Why not?"

"So how's your campaign with that cute new guy coming?" I asked as we drove back across town toward Burger King.

"Oh, only so-so." Tami shrugged. "The problem is he's really shy. But I'm working on that."

"I bet," I said. "In the meantime, how would you like to help me make sandwiches and potato salad?"

"Thanks, but no thanks. I think I'll stick

with a book and some popcorn. On a scale of one to ten, that at least rates a six. Spreading mustard on bread comes in at about a minus two."

"A fine, helpful best friend you are," I answered, laughing.

A few minutes later we turned into the small parking lot in front of Burger King. As we stood in line, trying to decide whether or not to break down and get a cheeseburger along with my fries, Tami suddenly grabbed my arm.

"Peggy, there's Lon. Over there." She motioned with her head. "He sees you. He's coming over."

I looked in the direction Peggy meant, seeing the familiar figure of a tall, good-looking boy sauntering down the aisle. As he came toward me, I made a comparison between Lon and Chuck Whitford, almost as if they were being superimposed one on top of the other.

Lon was taller, of course, with dark brown hair cut short in the latest style. I remembered Chuck's shaggy hair, and a warm glow spread inside me. Lon's face was slender, with classic bones and a lean mouth. Chuck's face was more square, his mouth wide and generous. Chuck's eyes were blue, like a summer sky; Lon's were cool green, almost the same color as the dark green soccer shirt he had on. His jeans were new, deep blue. I remembered Chuck's sneakers, their toes frayed, his faded jeans, and that horrible hot pink shirt with Diaper Dan printed across the pocket. By the time Lon came up, I was laughing at the comparison.

"OK, what's so funny?" Lon asked.

"Oh, nothing." I made myself stop laughing. "I was just remembering something that happened in class. It's too long a story to go into now." There was an uncomfortable silence that I wanted to fill and didn't know how to for a minute. I had a feeling he thought I'd been laughing at him.

"Have you come to treat me to a cheeseburger?" I offered.

He didn't think that was funny, but did finally speak. "Actually, I was wondering if you'd like to go roller-skating tomorrow night. Some of the gang want to go as a group. Why don't you come along and show them how great you are on wheels?"

Tami, standing where Lon couldn't see her, pretended to sigh and clutched comically at her heart. I made a face at her that Lon thought was meant for him. This was not turning into one of my better days.

I apologized to Lon. "Look, I'd love to go roller-skating. Really. But I can't!"

"What do you mean, you *can't*?"

We were moving up in line toward the counter. In a second I was going to have to place my order. Now was no time to go into a long discussion about my new business. "I've just got a bunch of stuff I have to do, Lon. I can't explain it right now."

"Hey, look," Lon said, moving up with me. "You don't have to make excuses if you don't want to go."

"Hey, you two!" the girl at the counter broke in. "You want to order something?" She snapped her gum. "If not, then maybe you'd let the guys behind you place orders, huh!"

I scowled. "What do you want, Tami?"

"Uh, just a diet Pepsi, please," Tami answered. I knew she wasn't ordering fries because Lon was still standing there.

"Make that two diet Pepsis," I told the girl.

"Small, medium, or large?"

"Small," Tami said.

"Medium," I put the correct change on the counter. "And with lids, please."

Tami shot me a how-come-we-aren't-staying look.

"We've got to go," I told Lon. "I went shopping, and I've got food in the car that has to get into the refrigerator before it thaws."

"Well, I'm going roller-skating whether you go or not," Lon said. "And I don't like skating alone." He turned to Tami. "Maybe *you* wouldn't mind putting up with me for one evening."

"Me?" Tami said in a kind of strangled way. Then she lowered her eyelashes. I suspected she was wondering how I felt about the whole thing.

"That sounds like a great idea, Tami." I gave her my blessing. Lon looked pretty pleased with himself.

"I'll pick you up around seven-thirty," he said and sauntered off.

"Come on," I told Tami, picking up the drinks from the counter. "I guess I really should get that stuff home before it spoils."

We drove silently for about two blocks before Tami broke the silence. "Listen, Peggy, I won't go out with Lon if you don't want me to."

"Would you rather sit home and read a book while stuffing yourself full of popcorn?"

"No, of course not."

"Then go." I shrugged.

"Well, listen, you know what I mean," Tami said.

"Go," I said. I didn't look at her. "I don't have exclusive rights to Lon."

"Well, I know," Tami agreed. "But you two have been together for a while. And—"

"Go," I said, cutting her off, sounding sharper than I meant to.

We dropped back into silence. I turned into Tami's street.

"I won't go," Tami said. "I'll tell Lon I have a headache, or something."

"Tami!" I pulled up in front of her house, putting the car in park and turning to face her. "Don't be ridiculous." I looked over at her, and it was if I were seeing her through a guy's eyes for the first time. With her short, softly curling honey brown hair and pert little nose, Tami Bartlett was definitely on the cute side. Funny, I'd known Tami since fourth grade, and not once had I ever given much thought to her being a rival. But now a small feeling of apprehension slid into the area of my stomach. "Just have a great time, huh!" Then I added, "And think about me at home making potato salad and sandwiches."

"Sure, I will." Tami grinned. "But only briefly." Then she was out of the car and standing on the curb, waving as I drove away.

After pulling into my driveway, I parked in the garage. Turning off the engine, I sat for a moment, going over the recent conversation between Lon and myself at Burger King. What should have been an easy conversation between us had nearly turned into a fight. We seemed to be on edge with each other lately. Or was it only me? I'd told Tami that my feelings for Lon had changed. I couldn't remember if I'd ever really liked him all that much. But I must have, or I wouldn't have started dating him in the first place. Sighing, I opened the car door, getting out so I could push the seat forward and start unloading all those brown paper bags.

I was so tired I thought I couldn't stand for another second. Flopping down on a kitchen chair, I plunked my elbows on the table and rested my chin on my hands. The clock on the stove read five minutes past eleven. Mom and Dad had already gone to bed. The house was quiet. The curtains on the window over the sink were drawn back, turning the glass into a black mirror. Looking into it I could see, reflected, part of what I'd worked to accomplish during the last several hours. Wrapped sandwiches sat neatly stacked on the counter ready to go onto the refrigerator shelves Mom had cleared for me. There were plastic bowls filled with potato and macaroni salads. And there were my cakes. Chocolate, of course, sheet style, frosted and waiting to be cut into squares and wrapped. Also, there was stuff I hadn't really done anything with except pack into boxes—oranges and apples and bags of potato and corn chips. I'd cut up the cake in the morning, I thought wearily.

Standing, I walked over to the sink to get a glass of water. I glanced at the image of myself in the darkened window and pushed the straggling wisps of reddish-blond hair from my face. My dark blue eyes appeared huge in the pale oval of my face, and I looked tired, I thought. For a moment I felt sorry for myself. What was I doing here when I could have gone roller-skating with Lon? He would be driving Tami home about now. Had they gone for pizza the way we had when we'd gone roller-skating together? Had Lon skated with his arm around Tami's waist? Was he going to kiss her good night? The questions hung in my mind.

I filled a glass with water, then started putting sandwiches in the refrigerator. I would definitely wait until morning to cut up the cakes. At the moment all I wanted to do was go to bed.

Chapter Four

In the morning, however, any trace of down feelings had vanished. In fact, I found myself singing as I drove to the plant where my father worked. The backseat and the trunk were carefully packed with all the food, along with something else, a surprise from my father.

When I'd come down to breakfast, still in my robe, I'd wondered why my dad had suggested that I wear my new bright red soccer shirt and white duck pants. It wasn't until I dressed and pulled open the garage door that I understood his request. Leaning against the car's dented fender was a freshly painted red and white sign that read: Peggy's Lunches.

Driving, I told myself how lucky I was to have such a great father. He might be strict in

43

a lot of ways, but the way in which he'd supported this entire venture, and had gone that extra inch with the sign, showed just how much he loved me.

I checked my watch and saw that it was fifteen minutes before the plant lunch hour. I was only about two miles away, but I stepped on the gas just a little. When I swung into the parking lot a bit faster than I should have, I heard the box with the bowls of salad bounce. I envisioned the potato and macaroni salads slopping together.

Because of the small weekend crew, the parking lot was only about one-third full. It was easy to find a spot near one of the two entrances of the building. I got out and began setting up, using the folding TV trays Mom had suggested I take to hold the food. When I was done, I went to the trunk to remove my new sign. That's when I saw something out of the corner of my eye that I simply could not believe.

About fifty feet away from my car was a van. Blue metallic. But it wasn't the van so much as the banner stretched across one side, Chuck's Chili Wagon. And standing next to the van, dressed in those faded blue jeans, grungy sneakers, and a neatly pressed, faded blue denim shirt, was Chuck Whitford.

I stood frozen, my hands still half pulling

44

the sign from my trunk. He stared back, and all at once recognition set in. A broad grin spread across his face.

"Hi, there!" he called. "Need some help?"

"What are you doing here?" I yelled, my hands still on the sign.

He was loping toward me. "I guess it's true," he said, halting in front of me. "Great minds think alike." He flashed the same wide grin again. "Looks as though we both came up with the same idea at the same time."

"Well, I know when I came up with mine," I answered coolly, thinking of how hard I'd worked all week. "Just when did you decide to copy me?"

Chuck's face took on a look of surprise.

"You heard me," I accused. "You obviously copied my idea. I don't know how. But that's what you did." Somehow, even as I said it, I knew the accusation was unfair.

"You know something," Chuck said, his eyebrows shooting skyward. "You're positively nuts!" He anchored his hands against his hips. "How could I?"

"Well—when—when we were talking last Saturday," I sputtered. "You know, when you were driving me home."

"Oh, brother! If I recall, what we did talk about was how to afford our respective cars, and I mentioned I'd love to go into business for myself. Which," he said as he jerked a thumb in the direction of his van, "I obviously did. You, on the other hand, just kept rambling on about baby-sitting. So, if anyone stole an idea, it was *you!*"

"Oh—!" I glared at him, trying to think of an answer that would freeze him to the spot.

"Hey, miss!" a brisk voice, deep and kind of gravelly, interrupted. "Are you going to sell any of those sandwiches? 'Cause if you are, I'd like one. If you aren't, I'm going back to work."

He was a heavyset, middle-aged man with graying hair and a face like Charles Bronson's.

"I said," the man repeated slowly as if I weren't too bright, "are you going to sell any of those sandwiches?"

"Oh, yes—yes, sir." I nodded. "I most certainly am." Glancing past the man who'd questioned me, I realized there were more men grouped around the TV trays that held my sandwiches and other stuff. I flashed a smile in their direction. "I'll be right with you." I turned back to flip Chuck a superior, guess-we-know-who's-winning-now glance. But he was already gone, hurrying back to his van, where a group of men also waited.

I started to scowl, but I didn't have time. Someone else was trying to get my attention.

"Do you have any bologna and cheese?" a slender man with thinning red hair asked.

Then someone else was asking for a ham on rye, and I found myself, with a surge of adrenaline, handing out sandwiches and spooning potato salad onto little paper plates and thanking someone for saying that my chocolate cake looked good. The money clanked and crinkled into my money box, and I hoped I was making the right change. I felt like an actress in one of those movies they speed up for comic effect.

Then it was over; the men were sitting or sprawled on the grass, eating their lunches. I leaned against the fender to catch my breath. I smiled, thinking what a terrific feeling it was to see all those men enjoying the food I'd put together. Then I noticed something that wiped away all my happiness. A lot of them were eating out of paper bowls, bright yellow paper bowls. What was it they were eating?

Chili!

They were eating chili, Chuck's chili! What with all that had been going on, I'd nearly forgotten what had happened. I swiveled around, and I stared at the parking spot where the chili wagon had been. All at once my triumph was gone, and I realized just how tired I was.

Packing up what hadn't been sold, which

turned out to be more than I'd expected, I wondered whether any of the food could be frozen and kept for the following week. Not much, I thought. A lot of it was perishable.

As I drove back to town, I kept thinking about Chuck. *Really*, I asked myself, *how could he have come up with the same idea at the same time I did?* Somehow I couldn't quite swallow that line he'd fed me, about how great minds run along the same path—or however it was he had expressed it. No, what had happened had to be more than some wild coincidence; it just had to be. And I knew *I* wasn't the one who'd done the copying.

Chapter Five

I was almost home when I realized I had to talk to someone. Driving past my own street, I turned in to Tami's and parked at the curb.

When she answered the door, she didn't open it and tell me to come on in. Instead, she hung on the door and hid behind it.

"Oh, hi, Peggy!" She was really acting strange. "I thought you were supposed to be out at the plant selling food."

"I was," I said, giving her a puzzled look. "But now I'm back. And I decided I had to talk to you."

"Oh!" She licked her lips. "What about?"

"Just things. Is there some kind of problem that I can't come in?"

"Oh, no!" She gave me a phony smile. "Well, come on in, then."

"Gee, thanks!" I gave her another strange look. "I thought you'd never ask."

"It's warm, isn't it? Want some iced tea?" she asked, heading toward the kitchen.

"Sure," I said, following her. I watched as she poured tea from the pitcher. She added lemon slices. "Want some crackers to go with it?" She reached for a box of Ritz.

"No, thanks," I replied.

"OK," she answered, putting the glasses of tea on a tray and absently adding the box of crackers. "Let's go out to the game room."

Tami had four older brothers. To keep them happy, her father had built this game room with everything he thought they might possibly like to have. There's a Ping-Pong table, a small pool table, a secondhand pinball machine, a couple of old video games he picked up at some auction, and a fantastic stereo system. I have to admit it's pretty neat. And Tami's brothers aren't the only ones who enjoy the room.

Tami and I curled up on the rattan couch. "Cracker?" She held the box out to me.

I took one but just held it. "What is it with you? You're acting positively weird."

"No, I'm not," she insisted, turning pink.

"But you tell me why you look as though you want to kill someone."

"Because I'd really like to," I answered with a growl. "Chuck Whitford is a sneaky rat."

"Oh." Tami let out a huge sigh and slumped back against the cushions. "Chuck Whitford. And I thought—well, never mind." She shook her head.

"What do you mean, never mind?" I asked, not really needing to know. "Did something happen you don't want me to know about? Something between you and Lon?"

"Listen, Peggy," Tami said, looking defensive. "You said you didn't mind if I went roller-skating with Lon. You did, you know!"

I nodded, keeping a straight face. "So, what happened?"

"Not much." Tami reached for her iced tea. "Really."

"Yes, it did!" I looked her straight in the eye—not actually accusing.

"No."

"Did—did Lon kiss you?"

"Not exactly!"

"What's not exactly?"

"Peggy." Tami's cheeks were still faintly pink. "I know you and Lon dated for a long time." She hesitated.

"All I want to know is, did he kiss you or not?" I asked.

"OK, if you put it that way, yes. But it was only a friendly kiss. Honest!" she said and paused. "It was, well, what happened next—I thought you might have heard. And that that was why you were here. You looked so angry when I opened the front door, I thought you might be angry at me."

"What happened next, Tami?" I asked the question with a sudden calm when I should have been feeling terribly jealous. I wondered why I wasn't.

"Lon asked me to go out with him again." Tami took a deep breath. "He said he'd had a great time and hadn't realized before what a terrific person I was."

"Oh!"

"I'm sorry," Tami said in a low voice. "And, well, I said yes."

"Hey, that's great," I said, shrugging.

"I won't go out with him. I'll cancel."

"Tami." I stared at her. "I said I thought it was great that he asked you out again."

"But—"

Jumping up I walked over to the Ping-Pong table and picked up the little white ball that was held down by one of the paddles. I started bouncing it up and down. My eyes felt hot. Was I going to start crying because of

Tami and Lon? I searched for the jealous feelings I knew I should be having. I couldn't find them. They simply weren't there. *OK, Peggy, I told myself. What you're feeling is more left out than hurt because Lon now prefers Tami. But that's all. There's nothing really left between you and Lon. What you're really upset about is Chuck Whitford. Face it, you've been daydreaming all week about him.* Reaching up, I wiped away an escaping tear. *Wow, Peggy, you are some kind of a jerk!*

"Peggy? Peggy, are you OK?"

"Oh, hey," I said, forcing my voice to sound bright. "Sure!" I walked quickly back to the couch and sat down next to Tami. Covering her hand with mine, I said, "Didn't I say go out with Lon? Didn't I say I thought things were cooling off between us? Well, this just proves it, doesn't it?"

"Then," Tami said hesitantly, "you really don't mind?"

"Tami," I said and smiled, "do I have to chisel it in stone?"

She sat staring at me for a second. "But I can tell that there's something still wrong."

"Oh, yeah," I agreed. "There is. It's what I came over to talk to you about. It's the reason I was looking so angry."

"You mean that Chuck what's-his-name.

So what about him? I thought you said you liked him so much?"

"Yes. Absolutely!" Jumping up again, I walked back to the Ping-Pong table. I leaned against it, crossing my arms. "Listen to this, if you can believe it. When I got to the plant this morning, he was there ahead of me. And just guess what he was doing?"

"I don't know." Tami shrugged. "I can't guess."

"He was selling chili, that's what!"

"So?"

"Tami." I shook my head at her lack of comprehension. "Don't you understand? Chuck Whitford stole my catering idea. He was out there competing with me."

"Chuck Whitford stole your idea?" She looked at me as if I'd just earned the padded cell award for the year. "How did he manage to do that?"

"Well, I have to admit I can't figure it out either. All I can think is that I must've said something that tipped him to the idea when he was driving me home last Saturday."

"Oh, that's not possible." Tami shook her head. "You didn't even think of the idea yourself until Saturday night."

"Just whose side are you on, anyway?" I demanded.

"Yours, of course. Listen, maybe it's just

54

some kind of weird coincidence. Things like that do happen, you know." She waved a hand as I started to interrupt. "Look, let's forget about *how* for a second. You said he was competing. But what he's doing is selling chili. How is selling chili competing with selling sandwiches? Frankly, I think it only shows there's a real need for the catering business. Competition is healthy. Free enterprise is what makes America great."

I couldn't believe what I was hearing. Was this the Tami who had tried to dissuade me from starting my business?

"Right now," I said, "I could use just a little less free enterprise."

"Did he really cut into your business?"

"Did he? Tami, you should see the back-seat of my car. It's half full of stuff I wasn't able to sell. And most of it is the kind of food I can't save. Which means I probably didn't make any profit at all."

"I'm sorry," Tami said sympathetically. "And after all the work you put in."

"You got it."

"Do you think he'll be back again next week? Maybe he'll decide you're too much competition for him and quit. But you're not going to quit, are you? How can you, with all of the money you owe your dad?"

"Speaking of your father." Tami and I

both looked up as her mother entered the room. "He's on the phone, Peggy." She gave me a knowing look. "And I'm afraid he doesn't sound too happy. I'd suggest you answer it. It's off the hook in the kitchen. Good luck," she added with a sincerity that showed, I thought, just how angry my dad had sounded.

"What's with your father?" Tami asked.

"He's probably furious. I was supposed to come straight home from the plant. I'm not supposed to use the car for socializing until I pay off my debt to him."

I stood up very slowly. It wasn't exactly like facing a firing squad, but close. Maybe I was being a little melodramatic, but—

"The kitchen's that way," Tami said pointing. "Just in case you forgot." Then, sounding almost exactly like her mother, she said, "Good luck."

In the kitchen I stared at the receiver for several seconds before I said hello.

Chapter Six

Pulling into the driveway, I said a silent prayer that Mom's car would be in the garage. Sometimes Mom is capable of softening my father on matters that involve me. But the garage was empty. I parked, took a deep breath, and walked into the kitchen.

"Well!" My father was waiting, seeming to fill the kitchen doorway. "Let's hear your explanation."

"OK, sure, Dad," I answered, pausing just inside the back door. "I have one."

"I'd love to hear it." My father leaned against the door frame. He looked casual, but we both knew better.

"I went over to Tami's."

"That's your explanation?"

"Not all of it."

"You know, of course, that you broke your promise, Peggy. For whatever reason you wanted to see Tami, you could have brought the car home and walked over. It's only four blocks."

"But it was important! I had to see her right away."

"You could have called me to let me know," my father said calmly and, I thought, quite reasonably.

"I'm sorry," I said.

"I'm glad," Dad said. "But saying you're sorry doesn't really cut it. The fact is, you still broke your promise. And, for what I can see, not a very good reason. You could even have come straight home and called Tami about this matter."

"It won't happen again," I said, appealing to him.

"I know it won't," Dad said, standing straight again and folding his arms. "Because your car is now grounded. It stays in the garage until you've found some other way of paying off what you owe me. Understand?"

"What about Peggy's Lunches?" I was so upset, my voice came out whiny.

"I guess," my father said softly, "that unless you can find another method of getting

58

your food out to the plant, the business is finished."

For a long moment I stared at my father, a lump slowly forming in my throat. Finally I mumbled, "Well, what's the difference? My catering business is finished anyway!"

With that I turned and slammed out the door. "So now," I yelled at the empty backyard, "I'll just go get those stupid sandwiches out of the car before they smell it up!"

By the time I lugged everything back into the house, my father was in the living room. I could hear him rattling his paper. As I shoved sandwiches any which way into the refrigerator, I noticed that there wasn't any cake. It had all been sold. Well, at least I knew I hadn't been a total failure. But it was small comfort.

Up in my room, I flopped down on the bed and stared at the ceiling. After a few seconds I decided I didn't want to stay dressed in what I had on because it was just a reminder of the lousy afternoon I'd had. I got up and yanked off my red shirt and white duck pants, which had a mustard stain on them that I hadn't noticed before. "Terrific!" I said out loud to myself. "I'll never get that out." And I threw the pants and the shirt into a corner of the closet.

I got out a pair of my oldest, softest jeans, put them on, and pulled on my old pink sweat shirt, the one with Snoopy surfboarding on the front. Suddenly I realized what color it was. Pink reminded me of Chuck Whitford. I would never like pink again. I yanked the sweat shirt off and stuffed it back in the drawer, taking out a turquoise one. I put that on and went over to curl up in the white wicker chair by the window.

Drawing my knees up, I rested my chin on them. *What an unfair world,* I thought. I was willing to bet anything that Chuck Whitford didn't have to go home and report immediately to his father. That never happened to guys. And next week he'd be out at the plant selling chili. Without my competition, he'd probably make a fortune.

I must have fallen asleep because the next thing I knew, I heard voices coming from down in the kitchen. *Mom must be home,* I thought. I couldn't hear what they were saying, only the low rumble of their voices. But I was pretty sure that my father must be telling Mom all about the terrible thing I'd done. I wondered exactly what he was saying and what Mom was saying back.

I found out about fifteen minutes later. There was a knock on my door, and my father called, "Peggy? Are you asleep, Peggy?"

"No," I called back.

"Can I come in?"

"Yes." I straightened out my legs. They were stiff from being in a cramped position for so long. I got up and went over and sat down on the edge of my bed as my father came into the room. He came over and sat down beside me. The edge of the bed sagged. My dad's heavy. He isn't fat; it's more muscle because he works out with weights every day.

"You left this down in the kitchen," he said handing me the little metal box I'd been using to keep my money in as I was making change out at the plant. "You shouldn't leave something like this lying around."

"In the kitchen?" I had to smile. I knew that the box was just his excuse to talk to me. "Who's going to steal something out of our kitchen?"

"Well—" He scratched at his bald spot, looking slightly uncomfortable. "You shouldn't get into careless habits. Not if—well, that is, not if you're going to be in business."

"But, Dad, you said—"

"I know what I said," Dad interrupted. "But your mother just finished bawling me out. She said that, as usual, I hadn't taken the time to listen to what it was you had to say. And that you wouldn't have gone to Tami's if it hadn't been for a really good reason." Picking up the box, he rattled it. "Sounds as if you made a profit."

"Afraid not." I shook my head.

"Is that what you meant when you said Peggy's Lunches was finished?"

"You heard me say that?"

"I'm not deaf." Dad grinned.

"Oh," I said, feeling sheepish.

"So what happened? Didn't anyone want to buy what you had to sell?"

I shook my head. "That's not it at all." And I went on to tell Dad exactly what had happened. I didn't elaborate about Chuck. I can talk to Tami about that sort of thing, but not my father.

"You mean," Dad asked when I'd finished, "you don't exactly know how much you did make? Didn't you count to see how much money you have?" He looked astounded.

"No," I admitted. "With so many sandwiches left over, I just assumed I didn't make any profit."

"I don't believe it." Dad frowned and shook his head. "Where's your account book?"

"My account book?"

"Yes, of course." He waved a hand. "A notebook, whatever it is you're keeping track of your profits and losses in."

"Oh, that," I answered, feeling dumb. "I haven't started one yet." I jumped up and ran over to my desk. "But I know how much I've spent so far. Here!" I pulled out the rolled-up grocery receipt from Grab and Bag.

"See," I said, pointing to the total at the bottom of the long slip of paper.

He grunted. "But how about the break-down of various items? You surely didn't use up everything on this list for today, did you?"

"No, of course not," I said, sitting down on the bed again. "The staples are on there, too. There's the mayonnaise, the mustard, the pickles, and the plastic wrap." I'd started trying ing to find the figures on the receipt.

"OK, Peggy," Dad said patiently, "let's do this right. Go get something to write on."

Half an hour later, with Dad's help, I had a section of my school notebook that had been divided into various columns with neatly printed headings into which I'd filled the costs of the items on the grocery receipt, as best as I could remember what they were. There were some things I couldn't remember, and we put those under the heading of miscellaneous. "We'll get rid of that column in a few weeks," Dad said. "Now for the profit side." He handed me the box. "Count."

I did, first separating the change into different piles: the pennies, the nickels, the dimes, the quarters, and the three half dollars. Then the paper money: the ones, the fives, and the two tens. When I'd finished, I entered the total in the income column. It looked kind of forlorn, just the one figure all by itself.

I held my breath as Dad and I both compared the one figure with the week's expenditures. When I looked at the final figure Dad printed at the bottom of the page, I winced.

"Eight dollars and six cents," Dad said. "You made a profit!"

"Eight dollars and six cents is a profit? Dad, I could've made that baby-sitting in one evening and not have worked my tail off to earn it."

"Well, it's a small profit, I agree. But it's a profit nevertheless, Peggy." He put his hand on my shoulder. "You've just learned one of the first lessons in business. Very seldom does anyone just starting out make money. But you're already one step ahead. Because, honey, you've actually made a profit, small or not. So I would say that Peggy's Lunches is well on the way to being a successful enterprise."

"I don't know, Dad," I answered, feeling depressed. "I don't want to disappoint you. But I don't see the use of keeping on. Not with the competition. There just isn't enough business for both Chuck Whitford and myself."

"Is this an example of the new generation

of women that you and your mother are constantly reminding me you are part of?"

Dad had neatly boxed me in. I couldn't possibly answer yes. I shook my head no.

"Well, then, why don't you show me how the new generation would react. After all," he said and smiled, "what's a little male competition? Surely you can overcome that."

I grimaced, biting my lower lip.

"Peggy!" Suddenly he grasped my shoulders with both hands and pulled me to my feet. "You're my daughter," he said sternly. "You're a Jenkins. And the Jenkinses of this world aren't quitters. Do you hear me?"

"Yes—Dad," I answered.

"Good!" Dad said loudly and pulled me to him in a bear hug.

I didn't know how I was going to work things out, but I did feel it was possible. Dad had helped me to see that.

Chapter Seven

I sat on the porch swing, one leg curled under the other, pushing the swing back and forth with my toe. I wasn't doing anything—hadn't planned anything. It was one of those lazy Sundays. I had on my grungy ancient cords and an old but really comfortable sweat shirt that Mom kept threatening to throw away.

The weather had turned cool overnight and had that definite autumn feel to it. It wouldn't last. I knew that in another week it would turn warm again, and we'd have two weeks of Indian summer. It happened every year. But the coolness was kind of nice for a change.

Out in the street some boy was doing wheelies on his bike, and Emily Knox, one of the kids I baby-sit for, was practicing on a new pair of skates she'd gotten for her birthday. She looked up, saw me, and waved. I waved back. There was a guy, about my age, coming down the sidewalk at the same time. He and Emily just about collided, but he dodged at the last second. I didn't recognize him at first. Not even when he came to our front walk and turned in. Maybe it was because of the way he was dressed that I didn't realize it was Chuck Whitford until he was halfway to the steps.

"Hi," he called.

"Wh-what are you doing here?" I was half standing, still half sitting, my foot caught under my leg. I yanked. My foot had gone to sleep.

"Hey, don't get up on my account," he said as he reached the top of the steps. His manner seemed to be casual because he nonchalantly put his hands into the pockets of his slacks. But his appearance was anything but casual. He was wearing a sky blue turtleneck sweater under a gray tweed jacket, and the charcoal gray slacks he had his hands jammed into were neatly pressed. The grungy sneakers had been replaced by polished loafers. And his hair had been neatly combed back.

I finally managed to get my foot untangled and stand up. It was tingling, and I wanted to stomp it on the floor to wake it up. But I didn't. "What are you doing here?" I repeated.

"Does that mean I'm not welcome?"

"Are you serious?"

"OK if I sit down?" He motioned with his head toward the swing. "Do you realize you have a no-parking ordinance on your block? I had to park three blocks from here. And these shoes hurt." He glanced down and gave the offending shoes a look that indicated they were hurting him on purpose. "I usually wear sneakers."

For a second I just stared back. I couldn't believe it. Here was someone who'd stolen my business idea, standing on my front porch telling me about shoes that were hurting.

"You mean I can't sit on the swing?"

"I guess it's OK," I mumbled. I wasn't being even halfway civilized, and I was beginning to not like myself. He came over to stand beside me. But he didn't sit. We stood for a minute, practically nose to nose. I noticed he smelled of Dial soap and something spicy. I also noticed that his sky-blue turtleneck matched the color of his eyes. "Aren't you going to sit?" he asked. "I can't sit until you do. It's not polite."

I sat.

He sat. The swing began to move at an angle. I stopped it with my toe.

I was suddenly aware of just how nicely he was dressed and how sloppily I was dressed. It made me feel very uncomfortable.

Chuck pushed against the floor with his foot, making the swing bounce. "You're making me nervous."

"I'm making *you* nervous?"

"Yeah!" He looked at me. "And I wish you wouldn't." He raised a hand as if to run it through his hair, then stopped as if he remembered it was combed. "Because it makes me want to just leap up and get out of here. But I can't. After all, I got dressed like this and drove all the way over here because I thought we needed to talk. And I can't do that if I'm halfway down the block. So, maybe, maybe you could stop looking as if you'd like to feed me to your pet alligator and smile just a little. Even a phony one would do."

I did smile. I hated myself for doing it, but I couldn't help it. For a second he sounded so sincere about that pet alligator thing, I almost laughed.

"Great!" Chuck smiled back. "You have a terrific smile. You know that?"

I closed my eyes. He was doing it again, being incredibly charming, and I was starting to fall for it. "OK," I said, opening my eyes and crossing my arms to show I meant to be serious. "I'm willing to discuss whatever it is you want to talk about. But I'm warning you, I still think you copied me. And I don't appreciate it at all. I worked hard all week putting my business together. So how do you think I felt when I was unloading my stuff and saw you there ahead of me?"

Chuck raised an eyebrow. "So you admit I was there first!"

"A technicality!"

"And you don't think I didn't work hard? Listen, I spent the entire week getting ready, too. And making chili the way chili is supposed to be made, which is the way I make it, isn't exactly as easy as spreading mayo on a couple of slices of bread and throwing on a piece of bologna."

"What about my chocolate cake?" I argued. "I didn't exactly whip that up out of some box mix!"

"I do remember that. I saw all those guys eating it, and it made me mad."

"Sort of the way I felt when I noticed all those guys eating your chili," I admitted.

"Worse." Chuck settled back against the swing, throwing one arm casually along the top. "When I got home and did my book work, I found out I'd made a huge profit. All of fourteen dollars and change."

"I made eight dollars and six cents," I confessed.

"See!" Chuck said, drumming his fingers. I could feel the vibrations in my shoulder. "That's why I came over to talk. As I was putting away all my leftover chili, I started thinking. And I concluded that one of us should gracefully back out and leave the business to the other. There just isn't the business there for two." He smiled. "So that's what I'm here to tell you."

"Oh," I said softly, looking at Chuck, then smiling to show my appreciation. "Now I understand why you came over."

"And it's OK?"

"Of course," I said. Well, it was. After all, it wasn't as if he couldn't go back to delivering diapers. I was sure he made good money at that. "And thanks for coming over."

"Well, I thought it was the only way to handle it," Chuck answered.

"But would you just tell me something? Because I've really got to know. Did I say something when you drove me home from the gas station that gave you the idea of copying me?"

His conciliatory look was gone. "You don't give up, do you?" he said as he leaned toward me. "I didn't copy you. If I'd wanted to copy you, I would have been out there hustling cheese-and-bologna sandwiches and chocolate cake. Listen, my married brother was the one who told me about someone being needed to cater lunches. He works at the factory part-time on weekends. He was standing around the water cooler when one of the managers started talking to one of the other guys about it."

"My father," I said.

"What?"

"That was probably my father your brother overheard. Dad's a manager out there, and he's the one who was asked to find a caterer."

"Oh, so that's how you knew about it." Chuck nodded. "Frankly, I was wondering how you'd come up with the idea. I mean, I honestly thought you'd found out what I was planning and copied me."

"I would never do something like that," I said evenly, narrowing my eyes. "That's not *my* style."

"OK, whoa!" He raised both hands, palms toward me. "Look, everything's settled, right? So now can we just be friends from here on out?"

"Oh, all right," I agreed, suddenly feeling just a bit silly about acting hostile again.

"Good. Then I'd like to get to the second reason I came over"—he paused—"before I lose my nerve."

"Second reason?"

"Right." His fingers crept over and

touched my shoulder lightly. "I've been invited to a party tonight, and I'd like you to go with me. It's casual, just a beach party, for everyone who worked at King's Beach this summer. We're allowed to bring dates. Listen, don't say no because you think you won't know anyone there." He squeezed my shoulder. "You'll know me. And you'll probably know some of the others. I'm pretty sure some of them are from Gardnerville."

His fingers were warm on my shoulder. I really did want to go with him. I liked him a lot—once I stopped being angry at him for copying my idea.

He took my silence for indecision—which it was, really, and tried to convince me it would be fun.

"There'll be hot dogs over a campfire, songs, a little dancing on the sand. Look, I know tomorrow's a school day, but it isn't going to be a late kind of party."

"Sure," I said. "I'd love to go."

He stood up. "Well, I'd better get going now." We walked to the edge of the steps together. "I'll pick you up at six-thirty. Wear jeans and bring a sweater."

"Should I bring anything else? Hot dogs? Cokes?"

"Nope. I'll take care of all that." He ran down the stairs, then paused and turned.

"But I'd change into a different sweat shirt."
He grinned. "I wouldn't want you catching
cold. It *is* kind of chilly out at the lake this
time of year."

He was already at the sidewalk before it
dawned on me what he was referring to. My
sweat shirt, the one Mom kept wanting to
throw away, had a huge hole right over the
middle of my stomach.

Chapter Eight

"**M**y father likes you," I said. I was sitting beside Chuck in his van as we drove through town on our way to King's Beach. "I can tell. He's always polite whenever I introduce him to anyone, of course. But if he really likes someone, he always has this way of shaking hands twice."

"I like him, too," Chuck replied. He was paying attention to the traffic, applying the brake carefully before we came close to the back of the car in front of us. I appreciated that. I can't stand guys who insist on showing off by tailgating as close as they can, then slamming on the brakes.

The afternoon had remained cool but clear. The sun was getting lower in the west.

Above it was a long, slim banner of a cloud, glowing orange and purple, like a bank of embers in a dying fire.

"You look nice," Chuck said, giving me a quick appraising glance as we came to a stoplight. "That emerald sweater's quite an improvement over your sweat shirt. I hadn't realized your hair was so red—anyone ever call you Red?"

I knew he was teasing, but my "no" left no doubt how I felt about that.

He didn't like makeup, either, he said, and I heaved a sigh of relief that I'd chosen gloss over my new burgundy lipstick. I'd wondered about perfume, too, and decided, finally, on my lightest cologne, which I only sprayed behind my ears. *He'll only be able to smell it if he gets close*, I thought, then wondered if he would.

We hadn't said much to each other since leaving my house. Funny how having a date with someone hinders your ability to speak. I felt shy. Was he feeling the same?

I slipped a glance at him, hoping he wouldn't notice. He looked nice, but different from the afternoon. Each time I'd seen him he looked different. His hair was almost back to its chaotic state, which I had to admit I preferred. His jeans were just nicely broken in, and he was wearing a bulky white fisherman's sweater, the sleeves pushed up. I noticed how tanned and muscular his forearms were. The sun coming in through the windshield turned the soft hairs covering them to gold, and I wondered how it would be to have those arms around me.

The fantasy slid away as Chuck said, "If you decide you're not having fun, just let me know. Give a sign and we'll leave and go somewhere else—maybe a movie."

"Oh, I'm sure I'll have a good time," I said. "I mean," I said teasingly, "I'm going to the party with you, after all, so how could I not have fun?" But I wasn't feeling nearly as confident as I sounded.

"Thanks for the compliment," he said, looking more pleased than I'd expected. He slowed the van, turning onto the narrow road leading toward the lake's one beach. King's Beach is the only sandy part of the shoreline; the rest is rocky.

The sun was much lower, the sky now a light mauve, with only a few streaks of orange left. Outlined against the setting sun was a wooden lifeguard tower and a small hut that, during the summer, served as the snack shack. It was closed now, boarded up for the winter. A fire had been built on the beach a short distance away. I could see the silhouettes of several people clustered around it.

Other people were walking on the beach, down near the water, and a volleyball game was going on—though in the near darkness, I couldn't imagine how anyone could even see the ball.

Chuck turned off the motor, and our silence was quickly replaced by the shouts and laughter of the people out on the beach. Chuck got out of his side of the van, then opened the back doors and pulled out a box of food. I got out and waited for him.

"Hey, you look great," he said again as he came up to me.

I smiled at him. "Thanks," I said.

He tucked the box of food under one arm, then, with his free hand, reached out for mine. We walked toward the silhouetted group around the fire. I stumbled slightly as we reached the sand, and he tightened his hand around mine. A ball of nervousness formed in my stomach. Why had I agreed to come to this party? Why couldn't Chuck just have asked me to go to a movie, or something? I hate first dates when you have to meet a lot of the other person's friends. It always makes me feel so stupid because I never really know what to say after the introductions are over.

We came up to the fire, and silhouettes turned into people. We stopped and Chuck put his arm around my shoulders in a friendly way. "Hi, everyone!" he said. Then, "Everyone, I want you to meet Peggy." He reeled off at least nine names, but I'd already lost track of most of them. I just bobbed my head slightly as each introduction was made, hoping the smile I had plastered on my face made me look at least sociable and not like some idiot Chuck had taken pity on.

"Sit down." One of the girls who was already seated on a blanket patted an empty space beside her. Chuck left to put the box of food somewhere.

"Thanks," I said, sitting.

"In case you missed it when Chuck was making the mass introductions, my name's Kathy. Glad to meet you," she added.

"Hi!" I said.

"I never can remember names when someone does that to me," she said and shook her head. "I just go totally blank, then spend the rest of the time feeling like a real nerd because I can't remember anyone's name."

"Right!" I answered, laughing. The ball of nervousness began to melt. "Did you work here this summer?"

"In there"—she pointed toward the closed snack shack—"sweating over a hot grill." We talked for a bit, and then another of the girls introduced herself as Gloria.

Chuck was roasting our hot dogs while I

talked. They were skewered on a long stick, already beginning to bubble, fat sizzling down their sides. Seeing me he called, "Hope you like them well done."

"Just as long as mine's not black," I called back.

"Well, they were only a little black," Chuck admitted wryly, licking the last of the mustard off his thumb.

"They were great, honest," I said.

"Really?" Chuck asked, looking down at my plate where half of mine was still left along with some potato chips.

"I'm stuffed," I said, trying to be diplomatic.

Chuck nodded as if there was no way he could believe me and reached for my plate.

He tossed it, along with his, into the fire.

"Take a walk with me," Chuck said, reaching for my hand and pulling me to my feet.

"Where?"

"To the van so I can get my guitar."

"You play the guitar? And you told me you didn't have any talents other than making great chili."

"Wait until you hear the collective groans when I come back with it." Chuck's voice was tinged with humor. "Then you'll *know* my only talent is cooking chili."

But as I was sure there would be, a scattering of applause greeted us when we reappeared at the fire. And as we sat back down and Chuck settled the guitar comfortably in his lap, people began calling out song titles.

"One at a time," Chuck replied, laughing. "Take a number." Then he looked over at me. "Got a favorite?"

"Uh—'Love Me Tender,' " I said, only because I couldn't think of anything else.

" 'Love Me Tender,' it is," he said, immediately strumming the first chord. The firelight danced along his cheekbones as he played. The sound was soft and mellow, the kind that makes you want to close your eyes and dream.

"Come on, everyone, sing," Chuck ordered in a voice as mellow as his music. No one did at first, but then someone began humming in a low baritone, then another joined in, singing alto, and soon everyone was singing. All those voices mingled with the gentle slapping of the water against the shore.

" 'Hey Jude,' " someone suggested. "Hello, Goodbye" was next. Then another song from a new rock video. Then some guy complained, "Enough of this stuff. How about 'Ninety-nine Bottles'?"

" 'Ninety-nine Bottles' it is!" Chuck

announced cheerfully and, without missing a beat, swung into the bouncy tune.

But along about sixty bottles, some people began getting up and drifting away in couples. By thirty-nine bottles there were only four others left besides Chuck and myself. He put a finish to the song with a strum across the strings. "See," he said, winking at me. "I told you I'd send people away in droves with my playing."

I laughed. Then suddenly he bent over me and kissed me on the mouth. It happened so fast that I had to ask myself if it had actually happened.

"Come on," Chuck said, grabbing my hand. "Let's put this away and go for a walk ourselves."

On the way to the van, Chuck asked if I was cold. I shook my head, but he put his arm around my shoulders all the same. It felt good there.

After placing the guitar in the van, we walked back past the fire. Some of the couples had returned and were huddled together, staring dreamily into the glowing embers or kissing.

The moon had risen. It wasn't quite full. I stared at it idly and wondered if it was on the verge of becoming full.

"It's waxing," Chuck said, so closely matching my thoughts that it startled me.

"How did you know that's what I was thinking?" I asked, slightly shaken.

"Easy. It's like I keep telling you, great minds—"

"Think alike," I finished with him so that we both broke into a kind of crazy laughter.

"I guess we really do," Chuck said, taking my hand and swinging it as we began walking again.

We dropped into a comfortable silence; the only sounds were the plopping of our feet against the wet sand and the lapping of the water. The moon painted the landscape a soft gray and silver.

"It's too bad we live in different towns," Chuck said, breaking the silence.

"I know," I said.

"You know I don't really know all that much about you." Chuck squeezed my hand. "What do you like to do when you're not taking aerobics classes or whipping up great chocolate cakes?"

"How'd you know about the aerobics?" I asked, surprised.

"Oh, that's easy," Chuck said. "When I first saw you, you were wearing pink tights and a pink sweat shirt with The Sweat Shop printed across the front."

"Oh," I said with sudden embarrassment, thinking of how I must have looked to him the first time he'd seen me, my legs in those pink tights sticking out from beneath my car.

"How is the car, by the way?"

"Just great," I answered.

"I'm glad. It looked in pretty good shape yesterday."

I didn't want to talk about anything that reminded me of what had happened Saturday. "What about you?" I asked.

"Me?"

"Yes, you. What do you like to do when you aren't bragging about your lack of talents?"

"We didn't finish talking about you," Chuck replied. "You seem to do a lot of bragging about your lack of talents, too."

"OK," I said. "And I don't brag. It's just that I honestly don't have any real talents. I certainly don't have any great musical skill. As for school, I think that, with my grades, I can just about make it into a state college. If I decide to go, that is." *Maybe I'll end up going to some famous cooking school, instead,* I thought.

"And?"

"Well, I used to be pretty good on a skateboard when I was about ten or eleven.

Now I roller-skate, and I'm pretty good at that."

"That's it?"

"I'm afraid so," I replied. "Sorry, I hate to disappoint you."

"You don't," Chuck said, putting his arm around my shoulders. "Believe me, you don't."

"So," I said, slightly flustered, "what about you?"

"I guess as far as school is concerned, I'm middle of the road, too. I'm good in the classes that interest me, but in the ones that don't, I have a hard time forcing myself to pay attention. I don't think it matters all that much, though. I'm not sure that I'm going to college."

"Really?"

"Really," Chuck replied. "It's not that I'm too lazy to make the grades I need to get in. I'm sure I could if I had to. It's just that I'm not sure college is that important." He shook his head. "Oh, don't get me wrong, I think it's important if you're going to learn a specific career, such as law or medicine or engineering. But, otherwise, I think you're better off going to a school that specializes in what it is you want to do."

"So, what do you want to do with your life?" I asked.

"I'm not really sure yet," Chuck admitted. "I know someone my age should have a plan, but I don't. As I told you, I do know that I want to have my own business. Only what sort of business, I don't know. Maybe I'll work for a couple of years. Then when I do find out what I want to do, I might go to a trade school. Or I'll take some evening courses to learn how to set up my books and something about business law."

"Seems to me you've done some serious planning already," I said.

"You mentioned state college," Chuck said. "Do you have a major in mind?"

"I guess I'm like you—" We had stopped walking, and I stood facing him, wanting to tell him about my idea of having a real catering business. But I wondered if he'd think I was silly. Would he laugh? I decided not to share my dream for a while longer. "I guess I'll just wait to find out what I want to do, too," I said.

Chuck didn't say anything for a moment. He was still looking at me, his head bent. I noticed how the moonlight was highlighting his unruly hair. "I know what I want to do right now," Chuck finally said, his voice low and suddenly rumbly. Slowly he began to pull me toward him, tilting his head farther down so that he could fit his mouth firmly over mine. It was the second time he'd kissed me during the evening. But this time I knew I wouldn't have to ask myself if I'd really been kissed. I'd remember it for a long time to come.

When he finally removed his mouth from mine, he didn't let me go, but hugged me closer with my head against his chest. I could hear the strong beat of his heart. "Now," he said, starting to let me go, "I think I'd better get you home. I don't want your father changing his good opinion of me."

Chapter Nine

Tami and I were sitting on the grass of the school courtyard eating lunch. It was Monday. The weather had done an abrupt change again. Indian summer had arrived, and I had taken advantage of the warm day and worn my favorite summer dress. Normally I wear pants. But that day I felt like being feminine.

"Something's different about you today," Tami said. "I'm not exactly sure what, but there definitely is."

"Maybe it's because I'm wearing a dress," I said and wondered if the way I felt about Chuck showed. Did love really make you glow the way romance books say it does?

Tami shook her head. "No, that's not it. Of course the dress looks good on you, though. Green's really your color. It's some-thing else." Suddenly she brightened. "Did something nice happen since Saturday? You were so down then." She snapped her fingers. "That's it, isn't it?"

I nodded, all at once breaking out in a grin.

"Well, what?"

"I'm in love."

"You're kidding!" Her mouth opened, then closed suddenly as her face fell. "Did you—did you and Lon make up?"

"Lon?" I stared at her, confused for the moment. Then I put two and two together. "No—no," I assured her. "I haven't even seen Lon since he asked you to go skating on Friday."

"Then who?"

"Chuck Whitford."

"Chuck Whitford?" She looked puzzled. "But on Saturday you were accusing him of all sorts of horrible things. You even called him a sneaky rat."

"I know," I said. "But that's all over now." I drew my knees up and hugged them. "Now everything's different." And I went on to tell her about how Chuck had come over to my house and graciously given the food business to me. I also told her about the beach party. But I stopped short of telling her that he'd kissed me. That was still sacred between Chuck and me.

"That's sure some switch. But are you really sure he meant he was letting you have the business to yourself?"

"It's true!" I assured her. "And isn't he an absolute doll for doing that?"

"Either that or a wimp," Tami remarked. "Scratch that comment. He doesn't sound like a wimp to me. Not the way you've described him. But what if he should change his mind?"

"Not Chuck," I told her. "You'll have to meet him. Then you'll see exactly why I feel the way I do."

"But that's not too likely, is it? Considering he lives over in Morton. And didn't I warn you about having any kind of a long-distance relationship? It just isn't practical. It never works out."

"Stop being so depressing, Tami," I said, letting go of my knees and reaching for the bag of potato chips that was sitting between us.

"Could be that someone should. It's not that I'm trying to bring you down, Peggy. It's only that I don't want to see you get hurt."

The next four days I spent either day-dreaming about Chuck or planning menus for Saturday. I'd taken inventory of what had been left over from the first day, concluded what hadn't sold well and what had. And on Thursday I went shopping with a new and more organized list. It was a hectic shopping trip because Tami wasn't there to help me this time. But in a way I enjoyed the tension. This was how it might be if I did ever open my own catering business. I was tired but full of excitement by the time I put everything away at home.

As I was sitting at the kitchen table afterward, a cup of herb tea in front of me, I began to feel strangely depressed. I couldn't figure out why, until I realized that I hadn't heard from Chuck since Sunday. When he'd said good night, he'd promised to call. True, he hadn't said when, but I'd more or less assumed he'd meant early in the week. Yet here it was late Thursday afternoon, and I'd heard nothing from him. Had something happened to him? Or had he, as Tami suggested, had a change of mind?

No—no—no, I told myself, *that couldn't be true. Think, Peggy,* I argued, *you've been so busy you didn't even think about this until now. Maybe Chuck's busy, too. Maybe he's delivering diapers again. Or maybe he's been busy looking for a new job.* Sure, that was it. And Saturday morning he'd come over, or at least call, probably to ask me for a date Saturday night.

By Saturday I was so convinced I'd be seeing, or hearing from, Chuck sometime during the day that I moved about the kitchen singing the first bars of "Love Me Tender" over and over again as I added the final touches to my new lunch menu.

I'd cooked a corned beef and let it cool, then carved it into thin slices, piling the slices onto rye bread spread with spicy mustard. I'd replaced the egg salad sandwiches, which hadn't gone over at all the first Saturday, with submarines, layered with lunch meat, cheese, onions, and coleslaw. Instead of bothering with potato and macaroni salads, I'd doubled up on the packages of potato chips and corn chips. And because the cake had gone over so well, I decided to try to go it one better with homemade brownies filled with walnuts.

As I drove to the plant, everything packed neatly into the back of the car, I began daydreaming about the huge profits I was going to make. Dad had been right. Every new business needed a little while to really get started, sort of a shakedown period. I was sure I'd had mine and was now ready to make money. After paying off my father and building up the necessary emergency fund he insisted I have, the proceeds would be mine to spend as I wished.

But on what would I spend them? I didn't really need clothes. While baby-sitting during the summer, I'd spent some of the hours when the kids were playing or taking naps, sewing. So I had a pretty decent wardrobe for school. And Mom, being a fantastic knitter, kept me supplied with sweaters that all my friends envied. Of course there was that red coat at Mervyn's I wanted. I could get that. And I honestly needed it.

What about my car? I could have its dented left fender straightened. But I'd kind of gotten used to it. It gave the car character.

Tapes, paperback books, magazines? Sure, a few of those, too.

But as I thought about those things, it seemed that if I spent my hard-earned money on them, it would be gone soon, and I wouldn't be able to really put a finger on where it had gone. What if I put it toward something important, like my future business, Peggy's Catering? I wouldn't be able to go to a real cooking school until after I'd graduated from high school, but I could start a savings account for it. And I could begin to collect gourmet cookbooks and practice the recipes. Maybe I could even invent some new dish that would someday make me famous. Like Peggy's Flambé Chicken or Steak Jenkins.

I was still so wrapped up in my daydreams

that as I first drove into the plant parking lot I thought my imagination was still at work. As I brought the car to a stop, though, I knew what I saw was in no way my imagination.

There was Chuck's van, taking up *three* whole parking spaces. The small banner that had been on the side was gone, replaced by a huge, gaudy, red, white, and blue one, with letters at least three feet high that read Chuck's Famous Chili Wagon. *Famous?* Who'd made it famous?

I saw red. Pushing down on the gas pedal, I burned so much rubber off my tires they were smoking. It got everyone's attention. And by the time I screeched to a stop near the van, there was a crowd forming. I didn't care. I was too furious to care. I leaped out of the car, not bothering to slam the door behind me, and stomped across to the van. I shoved through the crowd to face Chuck.

"Just what are you doing here?" I demanded.

"I could ask you the same thing," Chuck answered with a scowl. He was holding a ladle dripping with chili. "In fact, I will. What *are* you doing here?"

"I'm opening up for business," I snapped.

"Well, I already have!" Chuck said in a no-nonsense voice.

"But—you told me you weren't going to."

"And just when," he asked, "did I say that?"

"At—at my house," I stuttered. "Last Sunday. We were standing on my front porch." Behind Chuck I could see a couple of the men beginning to smile.

"If I remember right," Chuck replied, "We were sitting on your swing. And you fully agreed with me that there wasn't business enough for the two of us."

"Oh, that's obvious!" I answered, trying to control my anger. "The way I understood it, you were agreeing to give up and let me have the business. It was only fair. After all," I said, raising my voice for the benefit of the viewers, "you already have one career, delivering diapers to babies." This time there was outright snickering coming from behind Chuck. I noticed a flush of red begin to creep up his neck. *Good,* I thought to myself, *I've scored a point.* But even as I thought it, I didn't feel very good about it.

"Perhaps you don't understand the meaning of the word *career.*" Chuck's voice came out cool and even. "I told you I wanted a business of my own, that I didn't want to work for someone else. And this," he said, waving the ladle in the direction of his banner, "for the moment, just happens to be it!"

"Chili?" I stared. "We were talking about what you wanted to do after graduation."

"Did you ever think this kind of thing could turn into a real business?"

Something suddenly occurred to me. Forgetting about the men standing around us, I asked in a quiet voice, "Did you ask me to that beach party just so you could talk me into not showing up today?"

For a long moment Chuck just stared at me, his mouth opening, then closing again. The look of hurt and anger on his face was deep, and painful for me to see. "Do you honestly think I'd do something so underhanded?" he asked.

Right at that moment I should have said I didn't believe he could do anything like that at all. But instead I found myself acting as if someone else was in control. Pulling my shoulders up and sticking my chin out like a five-year-old, I answered, "Maybe!"

The flush had reached Chuck's face. "That does it," he said. He turned and jammed the ladle into the pot of chili. Then with a controlled voice, he looked at the crowd of men and very politely asked the nearest one if he preferred onions or crackers or both.

"I'm not finished talking!" I said angrily to Chuck's back.

He didn't answer. He took money from the

man for whom he'd dished out the chili and began dishing up the next customer's order.

"Chuck?"

"Onions, sir?" he asked the man.

"Oh—just forget it!" I yelled. I stomped back to where I'd left my car, the door still hanging open. "Oh, darn him!" I said out loud and slumped against the fender.

Someone tapped me on the shoulder, making me jump. I spun around. It was the man with the face like Charles Bronson. "Sorry," he grunted. "Didn't mean to startle you. But are you going to sell stuff or not?"

"Oh—oh, yes!" I pulled myself together. "Yes, sir, I am!"

Moving quickly I started pulling things from the back of the car to start setting up. "OK, Chuck Whitford," I muttered, "you're not the only one doing business today."

Chapter Ten

"A hot fudge sundae, please," I told the waitress. "With double fudge." She wrote my order down and went away.

As soon as I had gotten home that afternoon, I had called Tami and asked her if we could get together. We had walked to this ice cream place that wasn't far from where we lived.

"Boy, Peggy," Tami said, sitting across from me and smiling. "It's a good thing you don't get depressed often. You'd turn into something resembling the Goodyear blimp."

"I'm not depressed," I answered glumly. "I'm furious."

"Oh—OK." She nodded. "But you could've fooled me." Our conversation was interrupted by some kids from school coming over to talk to us. But Tami hadn't forgotten the topic. As the waitress put my sundae in front of me and set down Tami's diet Pepsi, Tami asked me, "Have you and what's-his-name had some kind of fight?"

"Chuck Whitford," I corrected her. "But the way I spell it, it's S-N-E-A-K-Y R-A-T." I jabbed my spoon into the center of my sundae, sending fudge sliding down the side of the glass.

"Correct me if I'm wrong," Tami said. "But isn't this the same guy who you decided was fantastic after all? I'm getting confused."

"I don't want to talk about it!" I jabbed at my sundae again.

"Are you trying to eat that or destroy it?" Tami inquired sweetly.

"Can we talk about something pleasant?" I asked.

"I think we should talk about what's eating at you," Tami suggested.

"OK." Putting down my spoon. I leaned across the table and told her what had happened.

Tami looked at me with sympathy. "I'm not going to say it."

"What? That you told me he could change his mind?"

"Thank you for saying it for me," Tami answered.

"And now that I have, can we please, please drop the subject of Chuck Whitford? I just don't want to have to think about him again today." I leaned back against my chair, picking up my spoon again.

"Sure." Tami took a sip of her diet Pepsi and shrugged.

"How are you and Lon doing?"

Tami looked as if she wasn't quite sure of my motive in asking the question. Was I reminding her that she was now going out with my old boyfriend? Or did I really want to know? She evidently decided I wanted to know and proceeded to tell me how really great things were between them. "In fact, we're going roller-skating again tonight. We've decided to practice and enter the next Best Couples contest."

Some part of me was glad for Tami, and I told her that. But I could not shake my own uncomfortable and angry feelings about Chuck.

I spooned up some whipped cream and was immediately sorry. It was too rich. "I don't know why I bought a sundae in the first place," I said.

"I don't, either," Tami said. She fiddled with her straw and then said, "Why don't you come skating with us? We're going in a group, so you don't have to worry about a date. There'll even be some extra guys. Maybe that's the best thing for you to do. You know, get out. Forget about your problems for one evening."

"Thanks for asking, Tami," I said. "But I don't think so. I'm really tired."

"What you have is emotional tiredness," Tami said, sounding a lot wiser than I expected of her. "What you need is some exercise."

My sundae was melting. "Let's go," I suggested. Then I added brightly, "You can tell me what you're planning to wear for the contest."

We paused to look at the window display in the boutique, then walked on. The air was soft and warm. Indian summer was still with us. It was going to be the kind of evening that should be romantic. And I was going home to watch TV.

"You know, Peggy, I've been thinking about the profit you made last Saturday—"

I tried to interrupt, but Tami stopped me. "It was a small profit, I agree. But like your father said, any profit at the beginning of a business venture is a good sign. And you told me you made a profit again today. That means you're doing something right. Why not just do more of whatever it is that you're doing—and try a couple of new ideas to attract more business?"

"If Chuck continues to be there, I don't see what good that'll do."

"Competition, dummy! You've got to beat him at his own game. That's what companies do. They compete, using different tactics until the company they are competing against folds up and slinks away. You can do the same thing to this guy's chili."

Was this Tami talking, the Tami who'd thought the business too much for me when I'd first told her about it? Now I was the negative one.

"Listen to me. I've made the best food possible. I've asked fair prices. What else can I do?"

"Lots! Just let me think for a second."

"And I'm about out of capital," I added. But she wasn't listening.

"Have a sale," Tami said. "No one can resist a sale. You'll have to get there first and string up some banners. That's what's important, getting there first—and advertising."

"He gets there first because he has to heat up his chili."

"Does he get the best parking spot?"

"Well—" I thought back to noon when I'd arrived to see Chuck's van parked across the three best parking places.

"See!" Tami looked at me knowingly. "Next Saturday you've got to outsmart him. What do you think?"

"Maybe you're right," I admitted, my enthusiasm beginning to grow.

"Of course I'm right! Listen," she said, "you came up with the great idea of Peggy's Lunches. Your only problem was that you needed a marketing adviser. And I'm it," she said proudly.

"Oh, Tami," I said and hugged her.

We walked on, turning down my street. I began planning the kinds of signs I could make. It was when I got to the point of putting together a list of the supplies I'd need that reality set in. I would need money. And, as I had just explained to Tami, though she hadn't heard or didn't want to hear, I was about out of funds.

"It's no good," I said, stopping to face her. "I can't afford to make any signs. I'm almost out of money."

Tami listened to me, although she was clearly exasperated. "Boy, Peggy! What do I have to do, solve all your problems? Just what do other business people do when they're low on funds?"

"I don't know," I said. "Go bankrupt?"

"No, dummy! They get a loan."

"And from whom am I supposed to get a loan?" I asked glumly.

"Your father. After all, he's the one who bankrolled Peggy's Lunches in the first place. Surely he wouldn't want to see you go under just because you needed a little loan."

I threw up my hands. "You don't know my father very well, do you? He may have given me the help to get started. But he also made it very clear that he was not about to carry me, that the business was strictly my responsibility."

"Then are you just going to give up, fold up, and hand Chuck Whitford your share of the business?"

"I don't want to," I said honestly. "Peggy's Lunches means something to me now."

"Then ask," Tami insisted. "Tell me, what's the worst thing that could happen if you asked your father for a loan?"

"He'd say no."

"Then, I repeat, *ask*!"

"OK," I answered, not really convinced, but willing to try.

"Now, don't chicken out."

Chapter Eleven

"I knew Dad would say no," I told Mom, who was standing at the kitchen sink, cutting up a chicken, getting it ready to fry.

I plunked my elbows on the table and stared unhappily out at the rain. The weather had changed as quickly as my mood.

"Well, honey," Mom answered me, sounding sympathetic. "I know how disappointed you must feel. But you didn't really expect him not to react that way, did you?" She began mixing flour and spices into a bowl. "When your father makes an agreement, he sticks to it."

"I know," I said and nodded. "I told Tami the same thing. But she said I should try anyway."

"And she's perfectly right." Mom began dipping the chicken parts into the flour mixture. "If you don't try something, you never know if you could have succeeded."

"You're talking in contradictions!" I said.

"No." She shook her head. "I'm talking in generalities. Generally speaking, it is always better to try than to give up. Even with your father. He *is* human, after all. And humans are sometimes given to change." She laughed to herself. "*Even* your father." Picking up a colander full of broccoli she came over to the table with it and set it down in front of me. "Here, why don't you cut this up for me. Working's supposed to be therapy for what ails you." Mom didn't say much, but her eyes and her smile showed she loved me and supported me in whatever I'd do.

"OK," I said and shrugged.

"So what are you going to do?" Mom asked as she pulled out the skillet she uses for frying chicken.

"I really don't know," I answered, picking up the knife and starting to cut. Somehow I couldn't bring myself to say the words, "I give up."

"What about that idea Tami came up with, having a sale? I think that's a marvelous idea. I know whenever I see the word *sale* I can't stop myself from investigating. And then I usually end up buying something."

"Well, sure," I said. "It's a good idea. But what am I supposed to sell if I don't have money enough to buy the stuff I need to have a decent sale? Unless," I said with a hint of sarcasm, "it's a going-out-of-business sale."

"Hmmm!" Mom gave me a you're-not-talking-like-the-daughter-I-know look. "How are you coming with that broccoli?"

"OK," I said, glancing down to see that I'd cut one stalk so far.

"You know, honey," she said leaning against the counter, "I wish I could help by loaning you some money. But that would be going against your father's wishes, and I just couldn't do that. You do understand, don't you?"

I finished the broccoli, and Mom disappeared into the service porch. I heard the freezer door open and Mom rummaging around inside it. Then she was back, standing in the doorway holding up a huge brown paper parcel. "Here." She held the package out to me. "It's not exactly money. But you can consider it a loan of sorts."

"What is it?" I asked, puzzled.

"Part of some poor deer," Mom answered. "Otherwise known as venison. Your Uncle Robert gave it to us."

"Venison?" I was still puzzled. "What am I supposed to do with it?"

"It's a roast," Mom said. "I never could bring myself to cook it. Somehow I think of deer as running free and happy. But here it is, so you might as well use it."

So with Mom's help and my own ideas, the following Saturday I was ready to, more or less, cook Chuck Whitford's goose.

I arrived at the plant an hour early. He wasn't there. I parked the car across the three spaces he'd occupied the last time. Then I got out the signs that I'd worked on all week and propped them up across the other empty spaces so he'd have no choice but to park in the back of the lot. I walked over to the grass to see the effect. I had to admit, looking at it from that viewpoint, that I really had something. I was still standing there, smirking with satisfaction, when Chuck's van pulled in. I pretended not to notice. But he did the same thing I'd done the previous week. He slammed the van to a screeching halt, leaped out, and came striding over to me.

"Just what is this?" he demanded, waving his hand in the direction of my signs. "You can't take up all those parking spaces."

"Sure I can," I said sweetly. "There's no law. As for what it is, read for yourself." I raised an eyebrow. "You can read, can't you?"

"Peggy's Lunches—Wild—Wild—Wild—Wild—Wild Sale." He glared back at me. "Just what kind of sale is a wild, wild, wild, wild, wild sale?"

"Well, I don't plan on taking my chothes off, or anything like that, if that's what you're suggesting," I said, giving him a haughty stare. Then casually glancing down at my watch, I said, "Oh, goodness, look at the time. I really should be setting up my food. My customers should be out any second." I smiled wickedly. "And I want to be ready for the stampede. So, if you'll excuse me, Mr. Whitford, every second I stand here talking to you is a second wasted."

The Chili Wagon left before I'd even finished selling. I noticed it driving out of the parking lot as I handed out one of the remaining venison pasties. Who would have guessed that something resembling apple turnovers, but stuffed with chopped deer meat, potatoes, and onions, would have gone over as well as they had?

The idea had come from one of Mom's cookbooks, which said that for hundreds of years in Europe pastry dough folded into an envelope and filled with meat or vegetables was how the men carried their lunches with them. Sort of an edible lunch box. And if

European men could eat them, then why not the working men at the plant? And so they had.

Driving home with the filled money box sitting on the seat beside me, I smiled broadly. *Let's see you try and top that, Chuck Whitford,* I thought.

But round two went to the Chili Wagon. Chuck fought back with Chuck's Chili dogs, complete with the works. And I guess he'd learned how to cook hot dogs without burning them because they sold like crazy.

I fought back the following week with fried chicken, Mom's style, cold and served with potato salad. Round three went to me.

Round four went to Chuck, however. Free desserts with the purchase of two chili dogs was that week's theme.

"I've got to do something spectacular," I moaned to Mom, dumping my leftover sandwiches onto the kitchen table.

"Not so much spectacular as inventive," Mom suggested. "But I'm afraid I don't have any more venison hidden away in the freezer. And, please, no more fried chicken. I don't think this kitchen can take another grease attack."

"Then what?" I picked up a limp sandwich and tossed it down again. "What can I do that's inventive? Besides," I growled, "what is

so inventive about chili dogs? Yet twice everyone's deserted me for those stupid hot dogs."

"Well, you have to admit he's managed to
come up with a new twist each week."

"I keep coming up with something new," I
insisted.

"I know," Mom answered. "And each time
you do you have to lay out more and more
money. I guess that might be part of Chuck's
secret to success, stick with one product and
make the best of it."

"I think I'll go consult with my marketing
adviser." I said.

"Who?"

"Tami."

"Congratulations!" I told Tami as she
showed me the tiny little silver cup she and
Lon had won.

"Well, it's not first place," Tami said. "But
we got free passes for one night."

"That's better than Lon and I ever did," I
said.

"Thank you," she replied. She stood up
and went over and put the cup back on the
shelf next to the stereo system. We were in the
game room. "Now let's discuss strategy." She
came back and sat on the couch.

"Well, that's what I came over here for," I
answered, looking at her hopefully.

"You know," Tami said, "I think your mom had something when she said you should stick to one product. I know you're making a good profit on the days that Chuck doesn't outdo you, but I bet you'd make an even bigger profit if you did what he does and sold just one thing. I bet Chuck is making enough of a profit on the days he beats you to keep him going when you're taking in most of the business. He only has to have one set of staples. And what he came up with in the first place was something that doesn't cost all that much to make. I mean, how much can a fifty-pound sack of beans cost for heaven's sake?"

"So you're saying I should stick to sand-wiches? Tami, that's what I did today. And you should see how many I have left."

"And what did you say it was he did today?"

"He gave free desserts away with every two chili dogs someone bought."

"Well, there certainly can't be much profit in that, can there?"

"I guess not. So?"

"So. It sounds as though he's getting des-perate." She grinned. "I think you've got him on the run."

"Really? You think so?"

"Really," Tami said leaning forward. "Now

here's what you do. Next week you have a major sale."

I started to shake my head in disagreement. I couldn't afford a major sale. But Tami put her hand on my knee to stop me. "Hear me out, Peggy. You have all the sandwiches left over from today, right?" I made a face, remembering the pile left at home on the kitchen table. "Well, all right," Tami went on. "Go home and put them in the freezer. Next week, offer nothing but sandwiches at half price. What else are you going to do with them? You don't even have a dog you can feed them to."

She was right. The following Saturday I made a nice, big sign and set it up in front of the car. Minutes later I practically had to fight off the crowd, and I was out of sandwiches in about half the time I normally took to make my sales.

When the last worker had left, I leaned back against my fender to catch my breath. That's when I glanced toward the chili wagon and saw Chuck leaning against the center of his van. But it wasn't because he was trying to catch his breath, as I was. He had no customers. I should have been jumping up and down and yelling about my victory. But I didn't feel like it at all. Chuck saw me watching him. Pushing himself away from the van, he came walking slowly across the parking lot. He stopped directly in front of me. Jabbing a finger in the direction of my sign offering sandwiches at half price, he demanded. "Just what is that about?"

"It's called a price war. Gas stations do it all the time."

"Can you afford to do that?" he asked evenly.

I shrugged. "If you can't stand the heat," I replied levelly, "stay out of this kitchen."

"OK," I reported to Tami that afternoon. "I outsold him today. But I also barely broke even. I'm going to fire you as my marketing director if this doesn't work. Not only that, but I'll have to declare bankruptcy. I still owe my father almost as much as when I started!"

"Peggy, just trust me."

I suppose I'll have to, I thought, *since I've run out of ideas.*

The next Saturday marked phase two of the Peggy's Price War.

"Two sandwiches for the price of one!" Chuck stared at me as if he'd suddenly discovered he was talking to Bozo the Clown. "That's the same thing you did last week when you sold sandwiches for half price."

"Not exactly," I said pleasantly.

Chuck nodded but didn't answer back

immediately. Instead, he folded his lower lip over his upper, stuck his hands in his hip pockets, and frowned, looking back at his almost full pot of chili.

"All right, all right. I admit you've got me." Taking his hands out out of his pockets and crossing them in front of his chest, he looked at me and said, "But I think you're probably in trouble, too. So why don't we have a truce long enough to have a business meeting?"

"A meeting?"

"Right. I'll even pick up the tab. Pizza. But it'll have to be the small size. That's about all I can afford at the moment."

Chapter Twelve

Driving toward Godfather's Pizza, I had a smile of self-satisfaction on my face. Tami had been right. Given the right amount of competition, Chuck had folded. Well, maybe he hadn't exactly folded quite yet. But wasn't that what this business meeting was all about? Certainly it wasn't the winner who called the meeting, was it? Yet, when I pulled into the lot behind the pizza restaurant and saw Chuck's van already parked, my confidence oozed away. By the time I had maneuvered my car into the space beside the van, I was actually scared.

The van was empty; therefore, Chuck was already inside. I turned off the car's engine and sat with my hand still on the key. I glanced at the vacant front seat of the van, and the memory of the night Chuck and I'd driven out to King's Beach came sliding into my mind. And, of course, the memory of Chuck's kiss wasn't far behind.

Letting go of the key, I slumped against the window and closed my eyes. How, just how could a kiss that had been so real ever have been part of a scheme to get me to give up Peggy's Lunches? Had I been wrong to accuse Chuck of using the invitation to the beach party to sway me into giving up my business? Could I have jumped to the wrong conclusion?

My eyes still closed, fragments of scenes involving the two of us began to swim around in my mind. There was our first meeting, with Chuck in that absurd hot pink shirt with Diaper Dan written across the pocket, a completely genuine smile on his face. Then the time he'd touched my shoulder and the feathery feeling of his fingers. The time we'd sat together on my front porch swing. And again, that kiss . . .

"Hey, in there!" Someone tapped on my car window. Jerking my head away from the window, I snapped my eyes open and turned to look directly at Chuck. "Did you fall asleep, or die, or what?" he yelled.

"I was just on my way in," I snapped, feeling stupid that he'd caught me daydreaming.

"Oh, sure, I could see that," he yelled, raising an eyebrow.

"Oh, never mind," I said, scowling. Reaching for my purse, I started to push down the door handle. But he beat me to it, opening the door first.

The inside of Godfather's Pizza is pretty, in a casual sort of way, with natural wood paneling, framed posters of Italy, and green plants hanging from every possible corner. Chuck ordered a small pizza with sausage and green pepper, as well as two medium Cokes, at the counter.

Handing me my Coke, he led the way into the center of the room, where there was a cluster of tables. He paused at one, then glanced toward the rear of the room. "Let's go back there," he said. "Business meetings should always be private."

The booths were the closed-in kind, with high, wide sides so that you felt as if you were in a room alone. Lon and I had eaten pizza many times in those booths after roller-skating or going to the movies. It had been romantic then. But this was Chuck. And this definitely was not a romantic date. I opened my mouth to insist that a table would be much better. Chuck, though, was already at one of the booths, sliding into one side. There wasn't much I could do other than follow him and slide into the seat opposite him.

Folding my hands, I put them on the table in front of me. Chuck looked at them, then up at my face for a long moment.

"OK," I ventured. "You're the one who asked to have this meeting. When does it start?"

Chuck surprised me by closing his eyes and sitting back in the booth. He didn't say anything for a second. "I guess I'm not really sure what it is I want to say first. I thought I did. In fact, I practiced all the way here. I've been thinking about all kinds of things to say to you for the past couple of weeks. But I don't think they're the kind of things I should say out loud."

"Oh!" I stared at him, feeling a bit stunned.

"Right!" He nodded.

"Well," I said back, "I guess I haven't exactly been thinking complimentary things about you."

"I can imagine."

"Can you?"

"Of course." He took a swallow of his drink. "Why should you? After all, we've been going at each other like a cat and dog."

After an awkward silence the pizza arrived. The waitress set small plates in front of each of us, then placed the pizza pan in the center of the table. "Enjoy," she said and left.

"Well, look," Chuck said, lifting a piece of pizza, the cheese stringing out across the table, "the way I see it, we're rivals, right? But that doesn't mean we have to act like complete enemies. I mean, we're just cutting our own throats that way. See what I mean?"

"Maybe it's just good business," I replied. I picked up a piece of pizza for myself. Catching the cheese strings with my finger, I put it neatly on my plate.

"Losing money is good business?" Chuck shook his head. "Now you're being a Bozo," he said, taking a big bite of pizza. "Good business is *making* money!"

I had my slice of pizza halfway to my mouth but put it back down again. "The only reason I'm not making money," I shot back, "is because you're there, taking half my customers."

"*Your* customers! Those are my customers you're talking about."

"Well, thanks for the pizza," I said, pushing away the untouched slice, the warm feelings for him I'd felt in my car long gone. I stood up ready to leave. "I don't think this is getting us anywhere."

Chuck's hand shot out, grabbing my

wrist. "Wait a second!" he demanded. Then, instantly, he relaxed his hold. "Please, Peggy."

I frowned at his hand still on my wrist but sat down again.

"This isn't going the way I intended it to go at all."

"Just how *did* you intend it to go? You tell me you've been spending all your time for the past couple of weeks thinking horrible things about me, and you expect me to just sit across the table from you and smile?"

Chuck let go of my wrist. "Did I say the thoughts were *all* bad?"

"N-no." Confused, I shook my head.

"Well, they weren't," Chuck confessed, his voice dropping several decibels.

"Oh?" My voice was equally soft. "What were they then?"

"I'm not sure I'm ready to tell you," Chuck answered. "For right now couldn't we declare a kind of truce so we can talk things out?"

"I don't see what's to talk about."

"We could compromise." Chuck was suddenly all business. "Look! We both could win. We serve good food." He smiled. "I've heard compliments about yours." He grinned. "And I know mine is terrific!" Seeing me roll my eyes, he said, "Hey, I've heard comments, OK?" He waved his hands. "But the thing is, we're both losing money when we should be making it.

You, you're slashing prices right and left. And I'm out there handing out Twinkies with every two chili dogs. I don't know about you, but my profits are in shreds."

I nodded my head in agreement.

"So," he went on, "what I'm proposing is that, instead of continuing to compete, we complement each other."

"How do you mean?"

"I mean that we go back to our original prices, which earned a profit for each of us, but in addition we cooperate by sending each other business."

"I don't think I understand," I answered.

"It's easy," Chuck said. "We can work it this way. Instead of giving away desserts, which cost me money, I'll suggest to my customers that they go to you for dessert. And you can sell corn bread, or crackers, or something with the suggestion that your customers come to me to buy some chili to go with it. Understand now?"

"I'm beginning to. But—"

"OK, forget it!" Chuck gave me a disgusted look and bounced back against the rear of the booth. He crossed his arms and, I felt, closed his mind to all further discussion. "I should've known!"

"Listen," I argued. "I didn't say no. You're not even giving me time to really think."

"What is there to think about?" His voice still had an edge to it, but his arms dropped to the table, and he leaned forward.

"A lot," I answered, suddenly aware of how close he was. A completely unrelated thought struck me, about how very blue his eyes were. Quickly I glanced down at my plate and pulled my mind back to business. "I suppose we could give it a try."

"But just for one week," I added, tapping the top of the table for emphasis. "If it doesn't work out, we'll go back—"

"Don't say it," Chuck reached over and covered my hand with his. "It *will* work." His palm felt warm against the back of my hand. Curling his fingers gently around the side of my hand, he turned it slowly so our palms were facing. "We'll make it work, Peggy."

The week passed in a crazy-quilt pattern of thoughts about my future with Chuck—bright, bold, happy thoughts, interspersed with gray ones. By Friday, though, I'd pretty much pushed the grays away. And by Saturday morning I was humming "Love Me Tender" as I drove toward the plant, a dozen boxes of soda crackers nestled on the other half of the front seat of the car.

Pulling into the plant parking lot, I saw Chuck's van already there. He'd thoughtfully parked so that I would have an equally advantageous parking spot about fifty feet from his. I drove into it and turned off the engine. Then I checked my hair and makeup in the rearview mirror to make sure it looked the same way it had at home. I'd spent an extra fifteen minutes making it look perfectly natural. I practiced a quick smile.

Getting out of the car, I brushed the wrinkles from the front of my new blue slacks and straightened the bottom of the red- and white-striped rugby shirt I'd borrowed from Tami. Then I took a deep breath and stepped around the car. I raised an arm to wave at Chuck, who was standing next to the open side of his van. At the same time something inside the van got his attention, and he turned away. Then I saw what it was. Two long, slender, tanned arms came out of the interior and draped themselves over Chuck's shoulders. Chuck put his arms into the interior, and a second later he was swinging the owner of the arms out of the van to stand beside him.

The rest of her was long as well. Her long legs were emphasized by perfectly fitting blue jeans, and her long, perfect blond hair fell all the way to her waist. I couldn't see her face, but I hoped she had a long nose to match.

My arm was still up in the air. I yanked it down. It didn't matter. Chuck obviously wasn't interested in seeing me. He was too busy being friendly with the girl, who now had her arms wrapped around his neck and was laughing in that way that can only be described as possessive. I could tell that much, even though I still couldn't see her face. I decided, then, that I didn't want to. Not ever.

Like a robot I turned to take things out of my car and set up. But I didn't get far before I realized I was having a difficult time. My hands were shaking, and my heart was pounding at about the same rate. I tried taking a deep breath, but the air wouldn't go past my collarbone. I blinked and found hot tears leaking out of the corners of my eyes. That surprised me. I'm not the type of girl to cry. Leaning my forehead against the top of the car, I closed my eyes. The tiny gray thoughts began crawling out from where I'd hidden them. I'd been used again—Chuck Whitford had set me up once more. And now—now he'd even had the nerve to show up with his girlfriend. I reached up to wipe the tears that had reached my chin.

Sounds began to reach me, the faraway slam of a door from somewhere inside the plant, a couple of birds having an argument over on the grass, and Chuck calling out, "Hey, Peggy." Finally I heard the scrunch of his sneakers as he walked toward me.

Naturally I did the only sensible thing. Reaching into the front seat of the car, I yanked out the boxes of soda crackers and flung them wildly in the direction of Chuck's approaching figure. Then I climbed into the car and slammed the door. I released the brake and shot backward, then put the gear into first, floored the gas, and turned in a squealing circle before I finally headed for the exit. Out on the narrow road leading away from the plant, I kept the gas floored, scaring myself almost half to death, but not really caring. Thankfully there wasn't another car on the road. Around a bend, banked by trees so I was out of sight, I slowed, finally bringing the car to a halt. I turned off the engine and sat there. *Good grief,* I thought. *I could have killed a rabbit or something. Even myself.*

My knees were shaking. *Stop it,* I told them, willing them to be still. Hearing a squeal of brakes, I looked up into the rearview mirror to see Chuck's van stopped right behind my car. *Oh, no!* I thought. Quickly reaching up, I tilted the mirror and looked at my own reflection. *Oh, no,* I thought again as I saw the black smudges under my eyes.

I was trying to wipe them away when I heard the door of the van slam and running footsteps. Then Chuck was at the side of my car, bending down, knocking loudly on the window. "Peggy! Peggy!"

With a last swipe at my smeared mascara, I turned and rolled down the window. "What do you want?" I growled.

"Are you totally, completely insane?" Chuck demanded. He was breathing heavily and looked scared, his face almost white.

I found I was breathing pretty heavily myself suddenly. "How could you?"

"H-how could I what?" Chuck's voice rose.

"How could you bring your girlfriend with you?"

Now he looked confused. "What girl-friend?"

"Her!" I motioned angrily backward, toward the plant. "That's who."

"Her?" Chuck shook his head. "You mean Gloria?"

"Whoever!" I bit my teeth together.

"Gloria!" Chuck said, as if saying her name explained it all. I stared back. "Don't you remember meeting Gloria at the beach party?" He suddenly smiled. "Gloria's no girlfriend. Oh, she's a *girl friend*, but certainly not a girlfriend." He smiled again. "For one thing, she's much too tall for me. For another, she already has a boyfriend. We're just bud-dies. We got to know each other when we worked as lifeguards at King's Beach."

I wasn't convinced. I don't know why I wasn't convinced. Sometimes when I'm really hurt, I just close my mind to what people are saying.

"What is she doing here with you today?" I asked, my teeth still clamped together so that my voice sounded strange. "I don't exactly see a need for a lifeguard."

Suddenly Chuck stood up. I thought he was going to leave. I wouldn't have blamed him. I was being the worst kind of shrew, not giving him a chance to explain anything.

"Can you either get out of the car or let me in so we can talk without my having to break my back?"

"I'll get out," I said, starting to soften.

As I leaned against the side of the car and looked at him, my angry self fought with the more rational me. "Will you just tell me why she's here today? You never needed help before."

"She's here for both of us, dummy," he answered, his voice suddenly filled with tenderness. I shook my head, not understanding. Chuck put a hand on my shoulder. "I saw her the other day and told her about what we were planning to do. And she offered to help. Listen, she's a nice person. And she's also great at persuading people to do things. So she suggested being a kind of pitch person for the two of us. She remembered you and said she liked you."

"Oh," I said, feeling small and pretty embarrassed about the way I'd acted, but still uncertain. "And—and she's not your girlfriend?"

"Peggy," Chuck said, looking deep into my eyes, "what did I say?"

"That—that she wasn't. But I saw her with her arms around your neck."

"Peggy," Chuck said, putting his other hand on my shoulder, "Gloria was being friendly. That's all. Now, when I put my arms around *your* neck"—and he did—"it's entirely different. And when I kiss you"—and he did—"you should know just how different it is." And he kissed me again. And I knew.

"Now," Chuck said moments later, "I think we should get back to the plant so we can conduct business." He was still holding me in his arms. "But, before we do, I think there's just one small business arrangement we should take care of first."

"What?" I asked, puzzled.

"I was going to bring this up later—after I knew how things were going to work out between us." He grinned. "But now I think I know. Ms. Jenkins," he said, suddenly sounding all business, except for the twinkle in his eyes, "may I suggest we join our business ventures? You know, the way other companies do." He paused, looking upward as if for inspiration. "We might call our combined effort *Chuck's* and Peggy's Fantastic Food."

"Or"—I paused as if I was considering his proposal—"we might call it *Peggy's* and Chuck's Fantastic Food."

Chuck paused, raising an eyebrow. Then he smiled, and bending his head toward mine, he said in a low voice, "Now shall we complete the merger?" I doubt that big business deals are handled the same way, but this one was sealed with a kiss that told me we were headed for great success.

We hope you enjoyed reading this book. All the titles currently available in the Sweet Dreams series are listed on the next two pages. They are all available at your local bookshop or newsagent, though should you find any difficulty in obtaining the books you would like, you can order direct from the publisher, at the address below. Also, if you would like to know more about the series, or would simply like to tell us what you think of the series, write to:

Kim Prior,
Sweet Dreams
Transworld Publishers Limited,
Century House,
61–63 Uxbridge Road,
London W5 5SA.

or

Kiri Martin,
c/o Corgi & Bantam Books New Zealand
9 Waipareira Avenue,
Henderson,
Auckland,
New Zealand.

To order books, please list the title(s) you would like, and send together with your name and address, and a cheque or postal order made payable to TRANSWORLD PUBLISHERS LIMITED. Please allow cost of book(s) plus 20p for the first book and 10p for each additional book for postage and packing.